LIEUTENANT TUVOK STOOD ON THE BRIDGE OF THE *U.S.S. EXCELSIOR . . .*

. . . a bridge that now existed only in his memories. Captain Janeway stood with him, her mind melded to his. To his left was the image of Captain Hikaru Sulu, commander of the *Excelsior.*

"Are we about to encounter the Klingons?" Janeway asked.

"Not exactly." Tuvok kept his voice low and gazed at his monitor as if looking into a crystal ball. "The Klingon moon Praxis is about to explode . . ."

Suddenly the whole ship was shaking. A crewman shouted, "I have an energy wave from two-four-zero-mark-six!"

Captains Sulu and Janeway stared at the viewscreen. Then they both shouted.

"Shields!" Janeway ordered, but the images around her did not react.

"Shields!" Sulu commanded, and the energy wave rocked the ship. . . .

Look for STAR TREK Fiction from Pocket Books

Star Trek: The Original Series

Star Trek: The Next Generation

Star Trek: Deep Space Nine

Star Trek: Voyager

For orders other than by individual consumers, Pocket Books grants a discount on the purchase of **10 or more** copies of single titles for special markets or premium use. For further details, please write to the Vice-President of Special Markets, Pocket Books, 1633 Broadway, New York, NY 10019-6785, 8th Floor.

For information on how individual consumers can place orders, please write to Mail Order Department, Simon & Schuster Inc., 200 Old Tappan Road, Old Tappan, NJ 07675.

STAR TREK VOYAGER™

FLASHBACK

A novel by Diane Carey
Based on FLASHBACK, written by Brannon Braga

POCKET BOOKS
New York   London   Toronto   Sydney   Tokyo   Singapore

This book is a work of fiction. Names, characters, places and incidents are products of the author's imagination or are used fictitiously. Any resemblance to actual events or locales or persons, living or dead, is entirely coincidental.

An *Original* Publication of POCKET BOOKS

POCKET BOOKS, a division of Simon & Schuster Inc.
1230 Avenue of the Americas, New York, NY 10020

STAR TREK is a Registered Trademark of
Paramount Pictures.

A VIACOM COMPANY

This book is published by Pocket Books, a division of
Simon & Schuster Inc., under exclusive license from
Paramount Pictures.

ISBN: 0-671-00383-6

First Pocket Books printing October 1996

10 9 8 7 6 5 4 3 2 1

Printed in the U.S.A.

Each time we make a choice, we pay
With courage to behold the restless day,
And count it fair.

Amelia Earhart
Courage

PART ONE

PART
ONE

CHAPTER
1

"ANTHRAXIC CITRUS PEEL, ORANGE JUICE, WITH JUST A hint of papalla seed extract. It's an experimental blend."

"The success rate of your culinary experiments has not been high."

Lieutenant Commander Tuvok squared his shoulders despite the fact that he was sitting down. He consistently resisted Neelix's offers to find some combination of live growth and replicated fruits and vegetables that a Vulcan would find palatable. Consistently resisted, yet continually returned.

The plume on Neelix's head caught the unforgiving lighting of the starship's mess hall and virtually flickered its pastel colors, making the Talaxian's mottled skin appear almost yellow as he tilted a bit to one side and poured his brew.

"Ensign Golwat tried some yesterday, and she thought it was delicious. In fact, she had a second glass. And she *never* has seconds."

"Ensign Golwat is Bolian," Tuvok pointed out with some irritation at the comparison. "Her tongue has a cartilaginous lining. It would protect her against even the most corrosive acids."

Taking on the attitude of a sad monk, Neelix requested, "All I ask is that you try it, Mr. Vulcan."

Tuvok eyed him, then eyed the coffee, sniffed it, took a tentative sip, and waited for his tongue to dissolve.

Coffee, with a flavoring of fruit. And a few other added aromas for which there was no complementary flavor.

"Impressive," Tuvok offered, registering a certain satisfaction through the stoicism of his Vulcan nature.

Neelix rocked on his heels and smiled. "I'll start squeezing that second glass. Breakfast is coming right up. Porakan eggs."

"Porakan . . . ?"

"The most flavorful eggs in the sector!" Neelix threw over his shoulder as he moved off. "Scrambled with a little cream cheese, dill weed, and a touch of rengazo. A galactic favorite."

In the galley, he began some orchestration that involved sizzling and popping sounds, and spoke through the portal.

"Now, these eggs were not easy to prepare. After we picked them up on Porakas Four, I had to sterilize them in a cryostatic chamber for three days.

And then each and every one of them had to be parboiled *inside* the shell with a—"

"Neelix," Tuvok interrupted, wondering how *each and every egg* was somehow different in the vernacular from *each egg* or *every egg,* "I would prefer not to hear the life's story of my breakfast."

"On Talax," Neelix went on, unfazed, "it's traditional to share the history of a meal before you begin eating. It's a way of enhancing the culinary experience. My mother was brilliant! She could make every course, every garnish, come alive like it was a character in a story. My favorite was the one about the crustacean who—"

His words were consumed in a tongue of flame that burst from his stove. Neelix jolted backward, arms flailing, then immediately recovered and snatched a towel.

Tuvok pushed out of his chair and hurried there, but by the time he arrived, Neelix had put the fire out.

"What happened?" Tuvok asked.

"Some sort of power overload," the Talaxian said, staring curiously at his stove as if it would explain if they remained patient. "I'm afraid it decimated your breakfast. This is what my mother would call a tragic ending."

Tuvok eyed the stove, but saw no other explanation. "Engineering has been making adjustments to the plasma conduits to accommodate a new energy source. It may have created a thermal surge in the galley systems."

"Janeway to Tuvok," the comm system said with a

faint crackle, implying there was indeed some problem in the systems. *"Please report to the bridge. Mr. Neelix, I'd like you to join us as well."*

"Aye, Captain," Neelix responded before Tuvok had a chance. He looked up. "What do you think is happening? Why would the captain want me to come to the bridge? Do you suppose she could've heard about my new coffee?"

"Possibly," Tuvok said, "although doubtful."

"Then something exciting must be happening!" Neelix chirped, gasping. "Let's hurry! A new discovery, perhaps! A way to get you and all your crewmates back to your own people! I do hope that happens for you all someday, Mr. Vulcan, I really do."

"Thank you." Tuvok realized his response was cool and rote, and immediately also realized that emotional beings required more sustenance for their empathy if it were to be nurtured. "Your enthusiasm for our hopes is most appreciated, Mr. Neelix. Of course, if we ever find a way home and you come with us, that will mean that you will then be seventy years at high warp away from your own people."

"Mr. Vulcan," Neelix said as they left the mess hall, "you *are* my people now. Let's go see what the captain wants, shall we? Do you think it will be something wonderful?"

CHAPTER 2

VOYAGER.

Of all ship's names, in all the oceans of the populated planets in the galaxy, of all fleets in all spacefaring, had there ever been a name so fitted to the vessel bearing it?

Kathryn Janeway had heard the name in her own mind and from her own lips so often that the sounds were part of her, living inside her clothing, as much within her as she was within the ship, and as dependent upon her as she was upon the vessel itself. She and it were symbiotic, islands nourishing each other, with no other land in sight.

And her crew's voyage was a long one, showing little hope of growing shorter. Thrown across the galaxy by some form of scientific magic, they were seventy years from home space. And that was at full warp.

Continually waylayed by searches for energy, for food, for ways to survive, and by the quirks of strange territory burgeoning with its own life, both mild and threatening, their journey grew longer and longer by the day.

Janeway settled back in her command chair and tried not to think about this, but that never worked. Now she was thinking about it even more. She'd made a vow to keep and pursue the Federation edict for Starfleet personnel—"to go boldly where no one had gone before, to seek out new life and new civilizations . . ."

But every time she did that, giving her crew a short-term goal with a chance for challenge and satisfaction, she set back their long-term goal of just getting home.

That was her dilemma. Let them grow old heading home as fast as possible, without challenge or mission, or give them the missions and the challenges and let them have some form of a life here, in the Delta Quadrant, with their goal of home just a backdrop from which she hoped they could be distracted?

She was on her own personal voyage that way . . . could she captain their lives as well as their duties?

Oh, well.

She tapped her chair's comm panel and forced herself back to business.

"Captain's log, stardate 50126.4. Long-range sensors have detected a gaseous anomaly that contains sirillium, a highly combustible and versatile energy source. We've altered course to investigate."

The last word echoed again and again. Every time they stopped to "investigate" something, they shaved a little more off their chances of reaching home before dying of old age.

But they had to get halfway there before they could get all the way there. Before the next seventy years would come the next five.

That was what she was looking at on the forward screen—an energy source for the next five years.

First Officer Chakotay moved aside as Janeway left her command chair and moved to join her department heads, who were clustered around a couple of monitors.

"Sirillium," Neelix uttered in his modified court-jester tone. Neelix was their resident resident of the Delta Quadrant. Native to this space, no one on board had tried harder to plunge into the daily life of the foreign ship's crew than he had. The crew didn't even take as active an interest in themselves as he took in them and their well-being. Sometimes he was the best thermometer of how they were doing, physically and mentally.

"Yes," Janeway responded. "And possibly large amounts of sirillium at that. If so, we're going to need to stockpile as much as we can. I'd like to convert Storage Bay Three into a containment chamber."

Neelix turned the banded pastel colors of his plumed head to her and looked quite like a disturbed chipmunk. "My pantry?"

"I'm sorry, Neelix," the captain told him. "You're going to have to make other arrangements."

"Of course, Captain." Clearly disappointed, Neelix complied, but not without mentioning, "You know, if I injected sirillium gas into my thermal array, it might improve cooking time."

"Yeah," Engineer B'Elanna Torres said with her Klingon rasp barking, "and blow up half your kitchen in the process. Sirillium is far more useful as a warp plasma catalyst."

She brushed back her straight brown hair and seemed to think she'd made the only reasonable case. Just as she was about to preen her technical victory, she was overridden by Lieutenant Tuvok's ever-precise enunciations.

"The gas can also be used to boost deflector shield efficiency," the ship's chief of security said, his stiff Vulcan demeanor giving particular substance to his words. Straight as a board, his posture alone insisted that his use of the sirillium would be best.

Amused, Commander Chakotay leaned toward his captain and murmured, "The vultures are circling . . ."

Janeway smiled. "Well, there's certainly no shortage of good ideas." She turned to Chakotay, and with that movement signaled an end to bridgeside debate. "Have all department heads submit proposals for sirillium usage."

Tuvok responded as his console beeped, then reported, "The anomaly is within visual range."

Janeway faced the main screen with anticipation. "On screen," she said.

A pretty section of space, the Delta Quadrant. Small comfort, but welcome. In her career she'd seen upward of a thousand gaseous formations, nebulae, thermals, clouds, spurts, novae, elephant trunks, and toxic soups, most up close and personal, and found that no two were alike enough to take casually. The privilege of seeing one of those had never been lost on her, until now.

Today she would gladly have traded the haunting blue cloud on the main viewscreen for a picture of Earth's marbled globe. As gas rolled, plasma boiled, and energy crackled within it and vibrant Bahama tide pools surged inside it, the blue of the nebula made her wish to see the blue of an ocean.

A pretty sight, yes, but barren of the life they all needed to see. It would help keep them alive and moving, but that was bare sustenance to a crew so very alone.

She sighed, then hoped no one noticed. To hide it, she glanced at her command crew. Chakotay seemed unimpressed. Torres and Neelix were inwardly fighting for control. That made her glance at Tuvok.

Yes, he too was hooked on that blue mass, staring with uncharacteristic attraction, almost as if held by some magnetic power. She almost commented, then forced herself not to. Vulcans didn't like to have their inner thoughts exposed, or let it be known that they had feelings down deep under the plaque of restraint. No sense embarrassing him just for a chuckle.

Well, not *usually*.

She looked at the screen again. "Analysis, Mr. Kim?"

Tactical Officer Harry Kim flinched as if she'd asked him to run out there and scratch the cloud with a fingernail to see if anything came off. He pulled his attention from the screen to his console. "It's a class-seventeen nebula. I'm detecting standard amounts of hydrogen and helium . . . and seven thousand parts per million of sirillium."

He seemed relieved to be able to confirm their find, and glanced at Janeway.

She turned away from him so he wouldn't see her accommodating grin, and found herself looking again at Tuvok.

He was looking down at his hand.

She looked there too. His hand was trembling.

A muscle spasm? Or was she seeing something else in his face? Was there expression in his eyes? Worry?

She'd seen him experience those before and instantly fight them.

He didn't seem to be fighting right now.

Again she walked the line of whether or not to call attention to his momentary lapse. She wouldn't want anyone calling attention to hers, but . . .

"That's the highest ratio I've ever encountered," she mentioned, just to hear her own thoughts aloud.

Torres stepped forward. "Captain, I recommend we use the Bussard collectors to gather the sirillium. They'll cut through that nebula like an ice cream scoop."

Gazing at the screen, Helmsman Tom Paris frowned in his pedestrian way. He was the only one who balked at the temptation of sirillium. "I'm reading a lot of plasmatic turbulence in there. It could be a bumpy ride."

Janeway forced herself to give that her attention for the moment. "Can you modify the shields to compensate?"

An automatic, normal question. Instantly she realized that the person who would be answering that wouldn't be Paris, but Tuvok.

When he didn't answer, everybody turned to look at him. Janeway realized she'd blown his cover.

"Tuvok?" She turned to face him. "Tuvok!"

His lips were parted, his dark skin pasty, and there was confusion in his eyes. Terrible confusion, laced with fear—Janeway knew that look. She'd seen it in the mirror. But never from Tuvok.

No, there was more. He looked ill.

Chakotay moved to Janeway's side and looked at Tuvok.

"Are you all right, Lieutenant?" he asked.

A tremor racked Tuvok's body. A glaze of perspiration struggled to the surface—witness to the stress he was under, because Vulcans rarely reached a point of physical stress enough to make them sweat visibly.

"I . . . do not know," he responded. "I am experiencing dizziness . . . and disorientation . . ."

Unable to clarify what he was feeling, Tuvok seemed embarrassed that he couldn't provide any answers.

He struggled for a few more seconds, then requested, "Permission to go to sickbay."

Janeway almost reached out to him, but held back. "Granted."

She almost ordered an escort for him, but knew that would be impolite, though probably prudent. He wanted to get away from their prying eyes, she knew.

She made herself hold back until Tuvok maneuvered stiffly, shakily, toward the turbolift.

The lift would do most of the work. Janeway found herself ticking off the actual number of physical steps Tuvok would have to take from the lift door to the door of sickbay. In her mind she walked every step with him. An ill Vulcan . . . no good.

"What was that all about?" Chakotay asked.

"Mr. Kim," Janeway said, turning. "Contact Kes in the sickbay and have her confirm when Tuvok arrives. I want to make sure he gets there all right."

"Yes, Captain," the young man said, but his hand was already on his comm panel.

Janeway was grateful for that, and heartened. They were beginning to really act like a bridge crew, anticipating each other's thoughts. That could only be good in the long run.

The long, *long* run.

"Very well," she said as if in agreement with herself.

Janeway stepped closer to the forward viewscreen, until she could feel the blue cast of the gaseous nebula coloring her cheeks.

"Mr. Paris, plot us a course into that nebula, right through the highest concentrations of sirillium," she said. "Nothing ventured, nothing gained. Shields up."

Lieutenant Tuvok clung to the side of the moving turbolift as if riding one of those carnival structures on some hedonistic planet, the kind upon which life-forms allowed themselves to be yanked about and driven at terrific speed until nausea arrived.

He didn't see the attraction. At the moment, even riding the lift was sickening.

"Help me . . ."

He snapped his head back and bumped the wall of the lift. He looked around—not his own voice. No one was here—

A female voice. Young. A child.

There was no child aboard this ship. Yet he knew he had heard a voice just now. The certainty, though, gave him no ease.

Anxiety crushed upward inside him—a terrible physical thing, as real as the nausea.

"Help me!"

He stared at the turbolift doors before him, at the straight seam where the two doors met, but the clear image began to blur before his eyes. Fighting for control with the fingernails of his mind as if clinging to a sheer rock wall—

Sheer rock wall . . . .

Rock.

He saw his own hand out before him, but it was an image from years upon years ago. His childhood.

"Tuvok!"

The girl's voice screamed plaintively, suffering in his mind.

But now it was before him, and he heard it physically, felt the open land around him, the outstretching mountains and plateaus.

Whump-ump . . . whump-ump . . . whump-ump . . .

Heartbeat. His own. The girl's. Faster and faster, he heard the sound of his own metabolism reacting to the rising anxiety, to the desperate screams of the girl.

Tuvok flinched to the core of his being as a face flashed before his eyes—a young girl, a Vulcan girl, staring at his eyes from a distance of no more than a meter—terrified. All Vulcan reserve had flushed from her eyes, and he couldn't help but react to that. Eight years old, nine . . . no more.

His knees flexed slightly as the lift eased to a halt and Tuvok heard the turbolift doors whisper open before him. He knew he had arrived at the sickbay deck. The Vulcan girl's face flickered and peeled away as the doors parted. The corridor before him seemed dark, cloying, as if carved from rock.

Rock . . .

Flushed with terror, he tipped his body forward as he let the ship's artificial gravity pull him out of the turbolift. It was as if this were his first walk down a starship's corridor, before he had ever gotten used to the unplanetlike, unequal tug of artificial gravity. After the first few weeks, such a tug became second nature, a thing to be ignored, like the slightly rich scent of artificially produced atmosphere, but at this moment he could feel and taste both as if he were a visiting *plebe*. His stomach roiled, and his legs were like tinder in wind. The corridor undulated before him like the gullet of some hungry animal.

Symbolism . . . nonregulation . . .

No logic in this. No female Vulcan child on board. No rock, no plateau. Still on board, corridor, sickbay. Forward, go forward.

Just as he thought he could regain control, a blanket of dizziness caught him as if by the throat, and he drifted sideways. If he stumbled, he would go over the cliff! He would die with her!

Panic tore through him as balance was knocked from his feet and he staggered. He crashed against something solid—the corridor wall had stopped him. He hovered there with his shoulder pressed against it.

No cliff . . .

But there *was* a cliff, there *is* somewhere. A cliff on board. The ship could fall off.

"Tuuuuvok!" A scream seared his mind. He heard it as clearly as the red alert klaxon.

He reached out and caught her hand, made a quick pull, and got her by the wrist. She was small, but her weight was too much in spite of that. Stones and slabs of shale cracked under her feet as she scratched desperately at the sheer rock wall. Dust plumed away, downward, spiraling in a rising thermal, forming a ghastly frame around the narrow body, the tribal clothing. Her pointed ears caught the rosy Vulcan dawn over the plateau. Her eyes were wide with panic on so intense and base a level that not even a Vulcan could bury a reaction. Death was final and frightening, and not even Vulcans could discipline it away.

He was too young to save her, too young to accept transfer of her *katra*—that was for her parents to do, but they weren't here. They were in the city, on business. She was entrusted to him, supposedly safe on this trail, on this plateau.

He willed all his strength to his hand, but his body would not give up his own grip on the plateau's edge. Self-preservation shot in and made him lean back just a few centimeters.

Enough—enough that the girl's weight shifted and bumped against the cliff face. Startlement and pain rippled through her body, up through her arm and into Tuvok's. Their Vulcan telepathic minds shared the terror she felt. If he could only keep moving against the turbolift wall, he could reach the security alarm and get help. A security team could pull the girl back over the top. Starfleet Security . . .

Please—

His hand cramped, knotted, began to hurt. He felt the girl's moist fingers slip into his coiled palm, then on through it.

Her feet flashed back and forth beyond Tuvok's sight of the girl's frightened face. She was kicking, panicking—

Don't kick—please don't kick.

Her weight yanked back and forth against his straining arm. Her fingers were wet and small in his hand.

Then a rare breath of wind came to caress his

wrist and take him by the hand, and his hand was
empty.

Peeling away as he watched, the girl's face
blanched with pure grisly dread as she fell away from
him, growing small against the rocky abyss.

And all he could do was watch her go, clutched by
the unkind emotions that thrived upon what had
just happened.

His lips hung open, sucking in and gushing out the
hot arid atmosphere of Vulcan, but now his teeth
began to ache with the fresh chill of starship-
controlled oxygen mixture. His clothing clung to his
skin as if baked on by the plateau sun.

His hands ached, his shoulder throbbed, his stomach lurched, and gruesome fright chewed at his mind
until he no longer could control the reaction of his
body and he shuddered viciously.

His hands—his hands—empty.

He staggered forward, and the gush of an entranceway whispered in his ears. He fell forward,
over the edge of the cliff.

CHAPTER

3

KES REACHED OUT TO TUVOK AS HE STAGGERED INTO the sickbay entrance, though she was small enough that he nearly knocked her over with his solidly muscular form.

As the ship's medical trainee, she knew nothing was supposed to surprise or shock her—the Doctor had told her over and over about maintaining distance and a certain medical coolness.

But Mr. Tuvok was shuddering with some kind of trauma, and Kes felt the trauma plunge into her own mind.

She was no Vulcan and could not use her mind's power to push away what she saw—a Vulcan boy leaning over her, his face pasty with terror, and she felt the terror fill her own chest and begin to pound and throb. The deck was gone under her feet. Her tiny slippers dangled pitifully as she kicked and kicked.

Tuvok!

She cried for help. Her voice was so high and thin! A child's voice . . .

One arm stretched out over her head, and he had a grip on that hand, but the grip was growing painful and weaker. He couldn't hold her! He was going to drop her!

She couldn't turn to look, but she somehow knew what lay below—unforgiving thorn bushes and jagged rocks. She'd pricked herself on those thorns before and scratched herself on those rocks. If she fell from this high plateau, the rocks and bushes would shatter her small body.

She was losing composure. A patient had come to her for help, and she was letting a vision take over. She had to help Tuvok—he was collapsing. His breathing was erratic, his heartbeat skipping, his eyes wide with the same terror as Kes saw on the boy's face.

She cramped her eyes closed and forced her semi-telepathic mind to refuse the image. She had never been on Mr. Tuvok's planet, so she couldn't be seeing it in her mind. She couldn't be hanging from a cliff. Something was wrong with Tuvok's telepathy, and it was encroaching on hers.

Please don't let me fall!

The commbadge on her tunic—if she could touch the commbadge, she could summon the holographic medical program, and the Doctor would appear and help her. Or she could call the captain for help, or Mr. Chakotay . . .

Neelix, help us! I love you, and you'll help me if you can. Come find us here and help Mr. Tuvok . . . please . . .

She raised her trembling hand, not the one that was clinging to the Vulcan boy's hand on the precipice, but the other one. She brought it to her chest and tapped the commbadge.

Something about the small movement within the cuff of reality shook her free of the terrible vision on the plateau's edge. Her eyes cleared as she opened them, and she saw Tuvok before her, on his knees, shuddering with effort and glazed with perspiration.

"Doctor!" she called.

Instantly the emergency medical holographic program popped into physical reality in the form of a studious and approachable man with a clipped, efficient manner, who didn't like unanswered questions.

"Kes! What's wrong with Commander Tuvok?" he said after seeing Kes kneeling on the deck with the Vulcan.

"I . . . I don't know . . . he came in the door and fell," she stammered. "I had a . . . he's having a . . . seizure of some kind. Doctor, we have to help him!"

"Of course," the Doctor said bluntly, taking Tuvok's weight as the Vulcan went suddenly limp and slumped into their arms. "Kes, what's wrong? You look deeply stressed."

She gazed at the helpless officer, who at any other

time was so strong and intimidating, and said, "I felt . . . I saw . . . no, nothing, nothing's wrong with me. It's just so awful for Mr. Tuvok."

"Kes," the Doctor said, flattening his lips, "you really must take more care to develop a medical composure if you intend to advance in the field. Professional distance is critical, especially in an on-board situation, where all of our patients will be people we know and work with on a daily basis."

"Yes, I know," she told him softly. "I'm sorry. I'll help you put him on the bio-bed. There's something terribly wrong, and it's hurting him."

"Obviously. I'll begin an examination. You notify the captain."

"Yes, I will. I'll do it right away, Doctor."

Tuvok! Don't let me fall! . . .

CHAPTER
4

"CAPTAIN!"

As the ship bumped to port, shuddered, then recovered, Kathryn Janeway plunged for the comm unit on her command chair as soon as she heard the medical trainee's voice burst through the link. That didn't sound good, and she knew just whom it didn't sound good about.

She suddenly felt as if she'd dumped her responsibility on someone else, and on such a gentle, delicate girl—shameful. She should've seen to Tuvok personally. Studying a gas cloud just didn't demand her personal custody.

Not even a cloud with an attitude, like this one seemed to have. As her hand hit the comm, she glanced forward at Tom Paris, who was dipping and ducking with the surges of the ship as he piloted through the unhappy gases.

"What is it, Kes?" Janeway asked.

"Captain, it's Mr. Tuvok! He staggered into sick-bay and barely made it in the doorway! He's having some kind of physical reaction, and it's very intense. I just happened to be standing there and I managed to break his fall, but I couldn't hold him. I activated the Doctor's program, and he helped me lift Tuvok onto a diagnostic bed, but now he refuses to tell us what happened. He insists on speaking to you. I'm sorry—"

"Not at all. Tell him I'll be right there. And, Kes, don't pressure him for answers until I get there. Have you administered any medication? Sedatives?"

"No, not yet. The Doctor prefers to, but only after you arrive. Mr. Tuvok is very agitated, Captain . . . I'm frightened for him."

Janeway felt as if there were two hundred decks between the bridge and sickbay and she'd have to hike every one of them. "I understand, Kes. Try to stabilize him, and don't do anything else."

"Yes, Captain."

Janeway clenched her jaw. That sweet, small-boned, big-hearted girl down there, faced with a shook-up Vulcan—how patently unfair. Since the ship's entire medical staff had fallen victims to the accident that threw *Voyager* into the Delta Quadrant, the ship had been depending on a holographic medical program and the goodwill and decent intentions of one Ocampa girl with a painfully short life span. Kes's short life span allowed her to learn very quickly—what choice did an Ocampa have?—but sometimes even a whiz had to handle things beyond her scope. An agitated Vulcan was way beyond almost anybody's scope, including another Vulcan's.

Certainly beyond mine, Janeway thought as she pushed away from the command center and caught herself on the helm. "Chakotay, I'm going to sick-bay. You can take care of this sirillium collection, can't you?"

The tall first officer gave her his reserved, half-devil grin, as if there were something hiding under the surface. "I imagine I can handle it, Captain. I don't envy you your choice of duties at the moment."

A vicious bauble sent the ship slamming to starboard as if it had struck a solid object. Janeway was still holding on to the helm, and Chakotay managed to stay on his feet, but at the upper console Harry Kim was caught with his weight in the wrong place and careened sideways into the subsystems console. He rolled from there to the deck, and lay sprawled for an embarrassing few seconds.

Chakotay looked to the upper deck to make sure Kim wasn't too badly bruised, then turned back to Janeway and added, "I hope Tuvok's all right."

"I'll pass that along to him. Keep me posted. And somebody pick up Mr. Kim."

"It was a chaotic experience, but my chief impression was one of . . . desperation. I was holding a young girl by the hand . . . trying to prevent her from falling into a precipice. I was unable to keep my grip . . . and she fell to her death."

Vulcan or not, Tuvok was still struggling.

He looked better now than Kes had described him when he staggered through the entrance to sickbay. The image wasn't very comforting as Kes told it, and Janeway believed her. Kes was gentle and sensitive, but she was accurate, too. Working with a holographic doctor all the time, she pretty much had to be.

Janeway stood beside Tuvok's bio-bed. Kes stood beside her. On the other side, the Doctor was running a medical tricorder along Tuvok's body and looking one hell of a lot more human than any computer-generated quick-fixer should look.

On the bed, Tuvok looked well enough, but only well *enough*. Few others might have noticed, but Janeway picked up on the tension he was working to bury, and though he often didn't meet the eyes of others unless he was making a report or an accusation, he now looked up at her and clung to her steady gaze as if it were a lifeline.

"And there is more." He struggled on. "I had an emotional response. Anxiety . . . fear . . . an almost irrational anger at myself for letting her fall."

"How do you feel now?" Janeway asked him.

He frowned unhappily. "It is a . . . distasteful but rapidly diminishing image."

"When did that happen to you?" Kes asked, probably not realizing how very stressful this turn of events really was for Tuvok.

She was a mild-voiced girl who, despite growing

old at warp speed, seemed never to change in her spritelike innocence. She even looked like a sprite, with puffy platinum hair and elfin ears. Add wings, and she could be a Flower Fairy.

"You said you were a young man," Kes continued, trying to help, "kneeling on a precipice. Did that ever happen to you?"

"It never happened," Tuvok answered, his brow furrowing with troubled thoughts. "The girl was unfamiliar . . . and I have never been in that situation." He paused to think, for the first time taking his eyes off Janeway and staring forward as if looking for something. "It *was* me as a child . . . and it did seem like a memory. But I do not recall such an incident."

He was frustrated, Janeway knew. The complexities of the mind weren't supposed to be a mystery to Vulcans, and when a dark cubbyhole opens up, it could be as disconcerting as recurring dreams to a human. Anxiety and fear were bad enough to those who were used to them. For a Vulcan, they were a vicious and punitive assault from within.

Janeway couldn't help but wonder about the little girl. Someone, somewhere, sometime had died. A child who never had a chance at the kind of life she herself sometimes bemoaned, and suddenly she didn't feel so very unlucky merely to be seventy years from home.

She wanted to put out her hand again to calm him, let him know she understood at least what he felt, if not why, but the Doctor completed his scan and lowered the tricorder.

"Well," the Doctor said, looking at Tuvok, "it was definitely a traumatic episode. Your heart rate accelerated to three hundred beats per minute, your adrenaline levels rose by one hundred thirteen percent, and . . . your neuroelectrical readings nearly jumped off the scale." The Doctor paused, then looked up from his tricorder. "If you were human, I'd say you had a severe panic attack."

"I am not human," Tuvok pointed out priggishly, with that sting of typical deprecation that Vulcans seemed to think was obligatory.

"No kidding," the Doctor said blandly. "I don't know what happened to you, but there can be any number of explanations." As Janeway tipped her head to listen carefully, the hologram went on. "Hallucination . . . telepathic communication with another race . . . repressed memory . . . momentary contact with a parallel reality . . . take your pick. The universe is a strange place."

Considering that this computer-graphic mock-up was walking around giving a diagnosis, Janeway had to agree.

"I'll have Mr. Kim examine the sensor logs," she said, looking down again at Tuvok. She felt obligated to say something, and since there was a handy gas cloud, why not start there? "Maybe our proximity with the nebula is affecting you somehow."

"In the meantime, Lieutenant," the Doctor said, "you're free to go. All your vital signs have returned to normal, and I don't see any residual systemic damage."

Tuvok tightened his body as if to get up, but the

Doctor moved in with some kind of small monitoring device and implanted it behind Tuvok's ear. The Vulcan didn't wince, but that didn't necessarily mean there wasn't a pinch or two involved.

"But," the Doctor went on, "I want you to wear this neurocortical monitor. In case you have another episode, it'll record a complete encephalographic profile, and alert sickbay at the same time."

"A wise precaution," Tuvok agreed. "Thank you, Doctor."

Tuvok stood up and seemed stable enough, but Janeway watched him custodially. She saw trouble behind his expression, just a wash of duskiness beneath his complexion, a crimp of worry behind his eyes.

Yes, he was deeply affected. Not having the memory evidently hadn't prevented him from living the experience, and now having to live with the aftershocks. Somewhere in the past a child had died, and Tuvok held himself responsible.

Had it happened? Had something so ghastly occurred in his past that he had buried the moment and forgotten the child? Was this one of the many mysteries of Tuvok that Janeway had yet to uncover, despite their long years of trust?

Someone else's past was always a strange zone to wander, and a Vulcan's was particularly private. Did she dare ask? Pursue the pain for him if he couldn't do it for himself? Would that do more harm than good?

Just how close friends *could* a human and a Vulcan even hope to become?

"Do you think you're all right?" she asked him after the Doctor and Kes moved away. "I can relieve you of duty for a day or so, if you think the rest would help you."

"I would prefer not to leave you shorthanded," Tuvok said, fighting down the strain he was under.

She smiled. "I don't think I'm shorthanded for scooping ice cream out of a gaseous anomaly."

He looked at her curiously. "I beg your pardon?"

"Just something B'Elanna said." Despite the protocols about not touching a Vulcan unless it was necessary, Janeway clasped his arm reassuringly, because he seemed to need that. "You're almost through with your watch shift. If you go to your quarters now and rest, you'll have till zero seven hundred hours tomorrow before anyone, including myself, will miss you. Take it as an insult if you like, but part of being in a Starfleet crew, or any crew, is to make sure you're not *too* indispensable. So get some rest and don't feel guilty."

"Guilt is an emotion," he curtly pointed out. "Vulcans do not experience emotion."

Tell that to the little girl on the cliff.

"Oh, yes," Janeway said. "I forgot."

Kes was young, she was alien to this crew, she was gentle and unassuming, but she was no fool. The episode in sickbay with Mr. Tuvok had somehow established a link, however momentary, while he was distressed. Somehow this link still remained.

She didn't know whether or not Tuvok had been aware of her connection. He had said nothing, hadn't looked at her with any more than the most elusive of glances, as if embarrassed. Could a Vulcan be embarrassed?

Now she was heading for Tuvok's cabin to make adjustments on his cortical monitor, knowing that she had volunteered too quickly, with perhaps too much anxiousness in her voice. Perhaps the Doctor hadn't noticed.

Vulcans were very private people, she had come to discover, and she promised herself she wouldn't mention the episode of the mind link, or tell him how it felt to be slipping and kicking, dangling over a cliff hundreds of feet from the ground. The memory of it sent a shiver down her arms.

And the terror began once again to creep through her mind.

Candlelight soothed his psyche. Perhaps this was the one concession Vulcans made to the idea that romance was comforting.

Dozens of tiny fiberglass rods caught the light and refracted it along the tabletop. Each rod was cool in his fingers, attracting the attention of his troubled mind.

Before him, the *keethera* grew rod by rod. The goal was to create a structure, but never the same structure twice. His mind was being organized moment by moment by the architecture of the house of little rods.

A simple device, remarkably effective. He had heard that humans tended to construct puzzles and miniatures of vessels for the same kind of mental result.

He closed his eyes and inhaled deeply, then slowly let the breath out.

"A house cannot stand without a foundation," he murmured. "Logic is the foundation of control . . ."

He placed another rod on the *keethera*, without opening his eyes, forcing his mind to see the structure's details without physical vision.

"Control is the essence of function . . . I am in control."

His fingers found another rod, and he raised his hand toward the structure. A nerve in his palm flinched—a child's hand in his, slipping—

The rod clicked on two others. The *keethera* shuddered and collapsed with a startling crackle.

Tuvok's eyes shot open, his concentration snapped. So many hours . . . failed.

The distraction of his door chime sounding was actually welcome. Visitors rarely came here, and the sound perplexed him for an instant, before he finally said, "Enter."

The door hissed, and Kes came in, holding a small medical device.

Tuvok stood up.

"Kes . . . what is it?"

The young girl offered him a comforting smile. She didn't seem to be as put off by his Vulcan nature as most other beings. In many ways, Kes was quite Vulcan in her steady manner, yet with the easy affability of a calm human. Interesting, because she was neither of those.

"The Doctor wanted me to adjust your neurocortical monitor to pick up additional peptide readings," she said. Then she paused, looked at him briefly, and added, "I can come back later if this is a bad time."

Most astute.

"No," Tuvok said. "You may proceed."

He sat down on his couch. Eyeing him with an undue hesitation, Kes slowly moved to him and systematically adjusted the device behind his ear, gradually enough that each added pinch could be absorbed with a minimum of discomfort. He appreciated her delicate touch, yet said nothing.

"What are you working on?" she asked, nodding at the jumble of tiny rods on the table.

"It is called a *keethera*," he explained, inexplicably embarrassed by the structureless pile.

"Keethera," Kes tested. "What does it mean?"

"The approximate translation is 'structure of harmony.' It is used as a meditational aid. Building it requires precise coordination and dexterity. It helps focus thought and refine mental control."

Instantly he realized that his explanation had just borne witness to his utter failure at focusing his thoughts.

"At the moment," Kes murmured, "it doesn't look very harmonious."

He glanced at her. She was annoyingly bright.

"No," he said. "It does not."

Kes finished the adjustment on his monitor and

turned to leave, then hesitated. "I'm curious. What does the *keethera* look like when it's done?"

"The form is not predefined. It is a reflection of the state of mind of the builder. It is different each time."

Again, he had just admitted his mental state to her, and was disturbed.

She smiled. "I'd like to see it when it's done."

Uneasy, Tuvok frowned and did not answer. This was an awkward moment, as he knew Kes was attempting to share his troubles and ameliorate them.

The sympathy in her eyes embarrassed him. She saw that, evidently, and turned toward the door.

"Kes," he found himself saying. When she turned back, he added, "I appreciate your attempt to improve my frame of mind. However, at the moment . . . it is a futile effort."

Her blond hair appeared particularly creamy in the muted candlelight. She paused, as if there were something she wished to say that caused her some unease. Finally her pleasant lips parted.

"I understand," was all she said. "Good night."

She did understand, and that in itself complicated his reaction.

With simple elegance she strode out. Somehow Kes managed to make a rather cool exit seem appropriate and warm. How did she do that?

Exhausted by the small exchange, Tuvok forced himself to sit again before the pile of glass rods.

He closed his eyes. Reaching out with one hand, he found the first rod.

"A house cannot stand without a foundation . . . logic is the foundation of control . . ."

Zero six-fifty hours the next morning.

"Morning" being relative.

Tuvok walked the corridor of the *Starship Voyager* with forced determination. The corridor pretended innocence, but there was something lurking behind the walls. He sensed it on a primitive level, and that alone was cause for suspicion. There was an identity at play here, and it was not his.

He disliked *sensing* anything. He preferred to know, to be sure, to have numbers and facts, to be able to prove. Handing the captain a report riddled with emotion and surfaceless concerns was inadequate. Appearing less than at his peak was inadequate. He had risen as far as he wished to rise on this vessel, for to rise higher would be to put Commander Chakotay and the captain out of their positions, or to rise there after they were dead, and he had no desire for either of those contingencies. He and Chakotay had their differences, but those did not as yet include sufficient stress for Tuvok to wish him away, or even to wish him the slightest ill.

He found himself relieved to have had that thought before Chakotay appeared beside him. Had a door panel opened and the first officer emerged? Tuvok had heard nothing.

Yes, the exec was now striding beside him.

"Mr. Tuvok," Chakotay bridged uneasily, "good morning."

"Good morning, sir," Tuvok responded, hoping his manner seemed much more normal than he felt.

"So . . . how are you feeling this morning?"

"If you are referring to yesterday's incident, I have not experienced any further problems," Tuvok responded, rather more sharply than he intended. "I am fit for duty."

As if he were part Vulcan himself and understood, or at least was trying to understand, Chakotay gazed at him almost warmly. "I didn't ask because I'm concerned about your ability to perform. I'm concerned about *you.*"

Tuvok bristled with embarrassment. "There is no need for concern."

Chakotay actually moved an inch or two farther away as they strode together toward main engineering.

"Sorry I asked," he offered.

Tuvok felt his brow tighten. He had worked among humans for decades now, and discovered that rudeness was all too easy for Vulcans to inflict if cautions were not observed.

And he had no desire to be rude. Not even with Chakotay, who obviously was making a gesture of unnecessary support.

Slowing his pace a little, Tuvok gazed at the deck for a moment, then looked up. "My apologies, Commander. I am distracted. I spent fourteen hours last night in deep meditation, trying to determine the source of my aberrant behavior." He hesitated a moment, then admitted, "I could not."

Perhaps as a kind of gesture of his own, he let some of his agitation show through. Perhaps he had no choice.

"Maybe you should try to forget about it for a while," Chakotay offered mildly. "I've found that when you don't think about a problem, sometimes the solution comes to you."

Being of Native American descent, Chakotay seemed to understand the value of cleansing the mind, pausing for thought, waiting for inspiration, or actively seeking it. Tuvok took that as a commonality between them, because at the moment he desperately needed one.

"It is difficult to forget," he said, "when you are wearing a neurocortical monitor at your parietal bone."

Chakotay offered a tolerant smile. "Good point."

For the first time, Tuvok found himself wishing the conversation with this former Maquis rebel leader could go on a bit longer. This vulnerability, which he saw as a complete negative, seemed to have its positive points. These humans empathized with him for this weakness rather than holding him in disrespect for his disability. They took weakness as a chance for strength. There was a unity among them in times of stress which Vulcans often dismissed as . . . silly.

It wasn't silly.

Not at this moment, when he felt a rare link with such a man as Chakotay. Could a good result come from such sensations of torment and guilt?

Guilt was illogical. He had let the girl fall to her

death, but he knew no girl of such description. The event had never happened to him.

Not that he could recall.

Such a chink in his armor was damning. He tried to resist the sensation as he and Chakotay strode through the main entrance to the engineering deck.

Together they crossed the deck to where Ensign Kim and B'Elanna Torres were studying a wall monitor that displayed a live exterior view of the nebula and fed out corresponding technical information about what the sensors were picking up.

"Mr. Kim?" Chakotay began, by way of jump-starting the moment and sifting for answers on Tuvok's part.

Tuvok was inwardly grateful, because he knew Chakotay and the others were studying the nebula as much for his well-being as for the rich sirillium deposits.

The nebula glowed on the small screen, and he felt his heart begin to pound.

"I checked all the sensor logs," Kim reported. "There's no sign of anything emanating from the nebula that would've affected Tuvok or *Voyager*."

"Anything unusual about the nebula itself?" Chakotay pursued diligently.

"No, it's a standard class-seventeen."

Tuvok found himself grasped by the vision on the monitor, unable to look away. The cloud rolled across the screen. Captain Sulu would know about such things, after spending so many years at the helm of a starship on deep-space exploration. This close to the Neutral Zone, there were many dangers.

A faint beeping in his ear . . . the neurocortical sensor . . . a buzz . . .

"We should conduct a tachyon sweep of the nebula," he said. His own voice sounded as if it were coming at him through water. "It would reveal the presence of cloaked ships."

Chakotay turned to him, concern creasing his expression. "Cloaked ships?"

"Yes," Tuvok clarified. "We should be extremely cautious this close to Klingon space."

They were all looking at him. He barely recognized them. They weren't part of this ship's crew . . . *Excelsior* had no female chief engineer, no Asian tactical officer . . . the captain was Asian, but . . .

"Tuvok," Torres began tensely, "the Klingon Empire is on the other side of the galaxy."

He looked sharply at her, but her image was blurry. He forced himself not to close his eyes or give away the trepidation he suddenly felt.

"Yes," he uttered. "You are right, of course. I am uncertain why I would make such an obvious error."

Chakotay took his arm. "Maybe you should go back to sickbay," he suggested.

Tuvok tried to answer, but he had made the mistake of turning again to the monitor, to the cobalt-blue cosmic sea through which they were passing at such intimate quarters. There was so much wind here, so much heat . . . anxiety coursed through his body again.

Again.

"Tuvok?" Chakotay's voice was far away.

Before his eyes were the girl's eyes now, wide and distressed, small feet flashing below in his line of sight.

She was slipping over the cliff's edge. He had failed to watch her, and she had ventured too close.

Now the wind had knocked her small body into a bow. Her arms flailing upward, her tiny feet lifting to their toes, then losing their tenuous grip upon the shaley rock—the maw of the abyss seemed to reach for her.

Tuvok cried out her name, but in his mind he didn't hear it. He *felt* it rip from his throat, to be snatched away by the plateau wind.

He plunged for the cliff, flinging his hand over the side barely in time to catch her tiny hand in his.

A furious hoist—he had her by the wrist. But no more than that.

She was so small. How could she seem so heavy? How could he be so weak?

"Tuvok!"

He winced at the piercing scream as the girl called his name on the breath of her terror. She was so small, only a child, entrusted to him for safekeeping, and he was failing. What would her parents say? What would his say? Would anyone ever trust him again?

She trusted him to pull her up. She knew she was dying, felt his grip slackening. The desperation in her eyes slashed him like blades.

"Don't let go!" she screamed. *"Help me!"*

His grip—moist, slipping—

He put out his arms to both sides as if to catch her from below. He tipped his head upward as if to see her fall and move beneath her.

And he kept falling over backward.

The child's narrow body spun toward him as he had seen flower petals disengage from their stalks and spin in the wind. He reached outward again, but the sky changed. The wind changed to a fresh, rich mixture. His clammy face turned cool, chilled.

The thing behind his ear whistled frantically. The Doctor would come soon.

He would come, and catch the girl.

Wouldn't he?

"The needs of the many outweigh the needs of the few."

Captain Spock
Star Trek II: The Wrath of Khan

CHAPTER
5

"Tuvok! Don't drop me! I'm going to fall over the plateau! Tuvok, hold on to me, please!"

"Please stop fighting me. I will try to pull you up."

"I'm—I'm hanging—you're going to drop me! I can feel my fingers slipping! You're losing your grip! Tuvok! Please don't let me fall!"

Her heart pounded, and her mind reeled with panic. Her fingers snapped as the bone broke in his last desperate clench, and as the pain shot down her arm and into her shoulder.

The sky turned and turned over her head, framing the Vulcan boy's head and shoulders and the one hand that was her lifeline. She should've listened to her mother and not come to the plateau today to play. Tuvok wanted to come here, and she wanted to do whatever Tuvok said.

She felt gravity tug at her small body and understood the science, but no one had ever explained terror to her, or that gravity could be terrifying. Her legs spun and kicked, her feet scratched at the face of the cliff, but she hadn't the strength to pull herself up, and Tuvok wasn't pulling her—why couldn't he lift her back up? He was supposed to be able to do anything. Couldn't males do almost anything?

As her finger bones snapped, her brain flew wild with pain on top of the fear, and she could no longer hold on.

Tuvok's eyes went wide as he realized the grip was finished.

She felt herself falling away from him. Her stomach jumped with the sudden moment of weightlessness as she went into free fall. Her arms flapped in useless circles, and she tumbled over backward. The thin clouds in the sky came to meet her as she fell, and fell more, and turned until she could see the jagged ground reaching upward like sharp-edged knives sloppily filed . . .

Medical files . . .

Kes clasped the Doctor's arm as he held her by the shoulders and kept her from falling over. Kept her from falling . . . she wasn't going to fall.

She was leaning back against a hard electrical trunk. Molded hull section. Carpet under her feet, not open air.

But she still felt the terror, her hand cramping as the grip began to slip.

"Kes, you're nearly in shock!" the Doctor said as

he scanned her with a medical tricorder. "Your heart is severely palpitating! What's doing this to you?"

"It's happening again! Tuvok—he's having another of those seizures!"

She felt herself shudder as the ghastly tale ran its course, and snapped just before her fingers slipped out of the desperate grip of the Vulcan boy.

"It's almost . . . it's almost over . . ."

The Doctor frowned with curious concern. "Are you in some kind of mental connection with Mr. Tuvok?"

She moaned as the last of the vision dissolved and she could once again see only the bright sickbay around her. Her head lolled for a moment, and she drew a long, steadying breath.

"It's over . . ."

"Do you believe you're in contact with him?" he asked again, determined to get any data she could give.

He maneuvered her to sit on an examining couch and immediately ran a bio-scanner along her upper body and head.

"No . . . no," she said vaguely, "not exactly contact. But that memory of the little girl came into my mind the same as it came into Tuvok's. I could feel what she felt as she was about to be dropped to her death . . . I could *feel* it!"

"You couldn't possibly have felt anything," the Doctor said. "You were here in sickbay all the time. So was Tuvok."

"But we weren't—not in our minds! Some kind of

a connection has happened between us. I don't understand, but it's true!"

"Not a complete surprise. As an Ocampa, you have some telepathic abilities," the Doctor pointed out clinically. "If his telepathic barriers are collapsing, he could be assaulting your mind without even intending to. Vulcans aren't very good at handling intense feelings, as we know." He stopped scanning and pinned her with a teacherly glower. "I should notify the captain about this, you know. I should also speak to Mr. Tuvok. Perhaps there's some sort of control he can exert over himself to keep from affecting you."

"No—" Kes reached out and caught his hand. "No, please, don't tell anyone. It's just a dream, some kind of illusion or vision. I can deal with it. If Mr. Tuvok is ill, he shouldn't have any additional stress put on him. This isn't hurting me, not really. Really, it's not."

"Not yet," the Doctor corrected, tucking his chin like a scolding uncle. "The captain has a right to know that an additional member of the crew has been put at risk."

She shook her blond head. "But I'm not at risk. It's only pictures in my head."

He raised the med scanner. "On the contrary, your heart rate and all bio signs are extremely elevated. You had a massive physical reaction that I cannot, as a physician, ignore."

With a so-there bob of his eyebrows, he started to turn away. "Sickbay to—"

"No, wait!" Kes called, leaning forward. "You can't tell anyone. You're not allowed to."

The Doctor paused and waited to see if that particular sentence were going to explain itself.

When it didn't, he asked, "I beg your pardon?"

"Your medical ethics subroutine," Kes said evenly, "should prevent you from breaching doctor-patient confidentiality unless I'm unconscious, and then only with next of kin. Isn't that right?"

The Doctor flattened his lips again. "As a matter of fact, it is not. Starfleet has never acknowledged the doctor-patient relationship as privileged for fear that withheld information could possibly jeopardize lives."

"Then do it for me."

"So you want me to withhold vital information from the captain?"

"Just for the time being. She already has so much to worry about . . . and Mr. Tuvok is so troubled. I assure you, Doctor, once we take care of him and solve his problem, I'll be fine."

"Agreed. But if the situation worsens, I may renege on our agreement," the Doctor said doubtfully. "Your reaction was a dangerous one. Your metabolism shot off the chart in every direction, completely overstressed, as if you'd had the fright of your life."

The Doctor seemed very dissatisfied, and for a few moments he was silent.

"I will comply with your wishes, Kes," he said after a few moments, "but if this happens again, I'll treat you as I see fit. If your metabolic rate shoots up as it just did, I'll sedate you and bring it down. Do you understand?"

"That's all right," she said, offering him a smile for a truce. "As long as you don't say anything to anyone else about this until Mr. Tuvok is out of danger."

"I've agreed," the Doctor clipped. "But I'm not happy about it."

as what did, I'll sedate you and bring it down. Do you understand?"

"That's all right." Tom, managing him a smile for a time. "As long as you don't say anything to anyone else about the way it felt. Tuvok is out of danger."

"I'll agree to that ... if you'll agree not to lie to your crew."

CHAPTER
6

"Tuvok!"

Chakotay automatically called out the lieutenant commander's name, but there was no shaking him out of what was happening to him. His eyes had gone blank, then filled with that horror they'd seen yesterday.

"Watch his head!" Chakotay grabbed for him and managed to shove Tuvok sideways enough that he didn't get brained on the console directly behind him. Together they went down in a heap, and Chakotay shoved himself up instantly.

"Not again!" B'Elanna Torres dropped to her knees beside the collapsed officer.

Chakotay knelt there too and made sure Tuvok had a pulse. The little cortical monitor was beeping and chirping desperately. Something disruptive was going on in Tuvok's mind, and there was no way to stop it.

He knew he wouldn't have to notify sickbay—the cortical monitor was already doing that—but the Doctor was a computer projection and couldn't come to Tuvok. Tuvok would have to be taken there for treatment.

"Kes might come now," Torres said, as if reading his mind.

Harry Kim stood over them, unsure of what he could do. "But he still needs to be treated in sickbay. I don't think Kes should be tampering with him, should she? After all, he's . . ."

"I know what he is," Chakotay said. "We should notify the captain. She's pretty protective of Tuvok."

He tapped his commbadge. "Chakotay to Janeway."

The captain answered so quickly it seemed she was expecting this.

Of course, she was probably expecting the report on the nebula.

"Janeway here."

"Captain, Mr. Tuvok's collapsed again. And he was looking at the nebula at the time, just like yesterday. It's got to have something to do with this."

"Something, but what? The color, the intensity, some field we're not reading? I don't like this."

"Agreed."

"I'm glad, but what's the report on that nebula? Where are you? Is Mr. Kim there with you?"

"Yes, we're in main engineering. Kim says the nebula is standard class-seventeen—"

He stopped and looked at Kim.

The young officer blinked, then spoke up. "Captain, it's class-seventeen, made of not much more than sirillium gas, dust, and ambient gamma radiation. It's just not all that unusual as nebulae go."

"Noted. Could it be emanating something that we're not picking up?"

Kim looked dismayed. "Um . . . there's nothing *in* there that could emanate anything. It's a very simple anomaly. In fact, the word *anomaly* barely fits it, now that we know what it's all about."

There was a pause of dissatisfaction from the bridge. *"Understood, but keep looking. Chakotay, transport Tuvok immediately back to sickbay. I'll meet you down there."*

"Aye, Captain."

"Janeway out."

Janeway would've preferred not to leave the bridge during this kind of maneuver, though this nebula they were passing through seemed relatively passive in spite of the bumps.

When she got to sickbay, the sight was disconcerting. Chakotay and the Doctor stood over Tuvok, who lay on one of the bio-beds, unconscious. Janeway was no medical specialist, but she knew enough about the medical scanner at the head of the bed to read that Tuvok was in great distress, his physical condition either severely depressed or overly stimulated. All the indicators seemed to be way up or way down.

"How is he?"

"Alive," Chakotay said.

The Doctor glowered at having the first officer put his two cents in where a medical answer was required. "His condition is stable, considering the level of agitation he's experienced. This time, the episode was far more than just a panic attack. You can see the graphic of his brain on that monitor to your left—representations of the axons and neurons are firing with general uniformity, except in this one area. This section near his hippocampus is firing very erratically. Clearly, something is quite wrong there. If you'll bear with me, I'll go to the med lab and analyze these data. Perhaps then I can have a hypothesis for you."

The Doctor looked at each of them, then actually sighed with a sense of inadequacy and headed out to the next-door med lab.

Janeway gazed down at Tuvok. He was unconscious, yes, but there was trouble on his face. Small muscles were tensed, and there was that glaze of sweat that showed a Vulcan was under severe stress. Vulcans could run a hundred miles and be tortured for hours without popping a drop of perspiration, yet Tuvok was drenched.

"Chakotay," she said. "Take the bridge. I'm going to go to engineering and look at Mr. Kim's analysis of that cloud until the Doctor comes to some kind of conclusion. I still don't buy that thing's apparent innocence. The only clue we have is that during both of these violent mental episodes, Tuvok was looking at the nebula."

"Over a screen," Chakotay said. "Technically, he was looking at a computer-generated representation of the nebula, not really the nebula itself."

"If I thought it would make a difference," she told him with a touch of irritation, "I'd send him out there in an environmental suit and have him look at it. But I don't think that would help. I'll contact you when I make a decision. I just hope there's one to make." She moved a little closer to Tuvok's unaware form and watched him twitch fitfully. "This is the worst kind of assault. The kind we don't know how to fight."

"You're a scientist at heart," Chakotay said, obviously trying to make her feel better against what he perceived as personal guilt that she couldn't reach out with a command order and solve this for her old friend. "You want data, anything concrete. These kinds of things are frightening to all of us, Captain. It's natural to want control."

"Still," she insisted, "he's a Vulcan. His brain patterns are very complex, but very orderly. If he passed out while looking at the nebula each time, that means there's a cause, a tie to the way that nebula appears to him."

"Well," Chakotay offered with a tiny smile, "I suppose we could just stop him from ever looking at it again."

She glanced at him, both aggravated and grateful. "If necessary. But that just means we're burying the problem. I'd rather get rid of it."

For her own comfort she touched Tuvok's forearm. Stiff, tight, even though he was unconscious.

"We're all alone out here, Chakotay," she told him. "And the few Vulcans in the crew are more alone than the rest of us. The others are content with their assignments, but in his high-ranking position Tuvok has to deal with everyone around him. He can't isolate himself as many Vulcans prefer to do. We've got to get to the bottom of this, or we'll have an unstable Vulcan on board to handle. I don't want that for us or for him."

Chakotay nodded. What else was there to do?

"Go to the bridge," Janeway said. "I'll be in touch."

"Aye, Captain," Chakotay sighed. Evidently he'd run out of reassurances.

He hesitated a moment, then sighed again, turned, and left the sickbay.

She understood his helplessness. He didn't like it any better than she did, even though he'd tried to talk her out of feeling this way. There was no Starfleet Medical Division to turn to, no neural specialists, either human or Vulcan, no advanced agency to consult, no infrastructure upon which to lean. They were all by themselves out here, with a holographic doctor who had all the galaxy's known data but no real experience with this kind of malady. And if there were decisions to be made, she had no one to turn to but herself to make them. There was no deferring to a wiser source, a higher authority. She was it.

Less than an hour later, she came back from engineering to the sickbay. She'd forced herself to stay down there, scouring the data on the blue cloud, and so far Mr. Kim was completely right about the damned thing. There wasn't a single hostile property, other than the few bumps and bruises it gave the ship. There were no readable emanations, not that anything could arbitrarily suffuse the ship's shields.

She came away from engineering angry, but she didn't know where to put her anger. What kind of an enemy was this? She wanted to reach out and wring its neck, but it was hiding.

If she could just get her fingers on it for a minute or two.

"Doctor," she announced as she strode directly into the med lab.

"Ah—Captain." The Doctor looked up from the monitor with Tuvok's brain scan on the screen. He seemed more hopeful, or at least glad to have something to report. "Mr. Tuvok is awake now and resting in relative comfort. He wishes to speak to you after I give you my report. I may have a theory for you to consider."

"Go ahead."

"I think we may be dealing with a repressed memory."

Janeway felt her brow pucker at those words.

But the Doctor moved again to the brain monitor, and she went with him.

"The memory engrams in the dorsal region of his hippocampus are being disrupted," the Doctor said. "It's causing physical damage to the surrounding tissue. In Vulcan medicine, this is known as a *t'lokan* schism. It means that the subject is inhibiting a traumatic memory which is beginning to surface."

"And that's causing brain damage?" the captain asked, determined to understand. Mental instability, maybe, but actual physical injury to the brain?

"Strange, I know," the Doctor agreed. "In human subjects, repressed memories are nothing more than psychological traumas. They can be dealt with through standard therapeutic techniques." He looked down at Tuvok with a sympathy and concern belying the engrammatic sense of life machines were beginning to possess. "But in Vulcans, there is a *physical* reaction to the battle between the conscious and the unconscious. In extreme cases, the mind of the patient can literally lobotomize itself."

The idea struck Janeway full in the heart, even though she had suspected something like this might be going on. Lobotomize itself! So powerful—and such desperation. The animal in the trap chews off its own leg. The terrorized mind commits suicide to avoid the terror.

Could Vulcans really be that different? Perhaps this was one of the reasons they strove so hard for control over their minds. A mind that strong was like a fire-breathing dragon on the loose. Control was essential, or it would self-immolate.

She was afraid of the answer, but she had to ask. "What's the treatment?"

"There is no medical treatment for this condition," the Doctor told her flatly, but with definite reluctance. "Vulcan psycho-cognitive literature suggests that the patient initiate a mind-meld with a family member . . . then the two of them attempt to bring the repressed memory to the conscious mind."

Pull the dragon forward out of the cave. Then kill it. Or tame it.

"Normally," the Doctor said, "this will result in what they call a reintegration. The memory is restored to its proper place in the conscious memory."

Janeway considered the idea. Again, the seventy years between this ship and home taunted her. "I'm the closest thing Tuvok has to a family member on this ship."

"That's why I've asked you to come," the Doctor said. "He has a request to make of you."

She stared at the Doctor for a long moment. She didn't have to be telepathic to know what that meant.

In the main exam area of sickbay, Tuvok lay on his bio-bed with his fingers steepled in concentration. He was strained, fatigued, his skin without luster, his eyes without ease. He didn't even notice Janeway approach until she was almost at the bedside.

"Did the Doctor explain the situation to you?" he asked. His voice had a telltale rasp.

"Yes," she said. "Tuvok . . . are you sure it's the right thing to do?"

He hesitated in frustration. The last couple of days had taken a bitter toll, both physically and emotionally, for him, and the stress was showing in his face, his voice, and how much this request was disturbing him.

"I do not know how else to proceed," he admitted.

"The Doctor tells me this is a memory, and yet . . . no matter how hard I try, I *cannot* remember it."

He took a steadying breath and tried to center himself, to regain control enough at least to discuss the illogical logically. Janeway gave him the moment.

"If the Doctor is correct," he went on, "if this is an experience which I have pushed into my unconscious mind, it could be very dangerous to me. Even life-threatening."

"But there's more, isn't there?" she asked, stepping a little forward against the bedside. "A little girl died."

Pain—emotional pain and guilt—crossed Tuvok's face. Janeway knew she'd rung the right bell.

"Yes," he uttered. "A child died. And if I am indeed the individual who allowed her to die, or at least who was present and unable to prevent her death, I have a responsibility to her family to stand before them and explain what happened. Yet . . . I have no idea who she was."

"A child doesn't just die in a vacuum," Janeway pointed out. "If there was a death, there must've been an investigation, a funeral, talk about it, awareness of it—don't you recall anything like that? You say the child called you by name, so she knew you, she wasn't a stranger. You must have some acquaintance with someone else who knew her or was related to her. This incident can't be all that isolated. But you have no memory of anyone talking to you about it, asking you what happened, no follow-up, no parents, no funeral? Am I right about this?"

"You are quite correct. I had not . . . considered those extrapolations."

That struck Janeway as quite odd. It showed her how much Tuvok's thoughts were being taken over by this, or perhaps that damage was already occurring. A Vulcan who hadn't considered all the extrapolations wasn't a fully operational Vulcan.

He seemed embarrassed that he hadn't thought of this, and confused all over again now.

Janeway felt bad, because she hadn't meant to confuse him, but she needed those answers. Was this image in his mind real or not? Had a Vulcan child died? Then why hadn't there been any question? Any funeral? Any mention of her later in his life? Such things just didn't happen and then never come up again.

Even in a glance, a whispered reference, a buried article—something. No one, not even Vulcans, could, or would, try to conquer tragedy with utter silence.

Even that, even the silence, would have said something.

"We'll do whatever is necessary to get this off you," she said. "Whatever happened, you shouldn't have to live with this. Accidents happen. Tragedies happen. It's all over, has been for decades, and there's no reason you should have to live under the weight of it."

Tuvok seemed comforted by her commitment. "I realize it is asking a great deal from you, Captain," he said, "and I did consider turning to one of the other Vulcans on the ship. But this meld is more intimate than most. A family member is normally chosen because of the implicit trust that usually exists."

He had been staring forward, avoiding her eyes, but now he looked directly at her.

"On this ship," he finished, "I trust *you* more than anyone else."

If he was admitting anything too deeply private, he was being driven to do so by the turmoil Janeway read behind his eyes. She was glad of that turmoil just for a moment, so they would be completely honest and drop all the shields of propriety and privacy and dig for the core of the trouble.

She had to find her enemy. Find it, then fight it.

"Whatever happens, I'll be there for you, Tuvok," she said. "I'll help you get through this."

He gazed at her almost warmly. "I will initiate the meld, and attempt to access the memory fragment of the girl and the cliffside. Once that has been accomplished, you will act as my *pyllora.*"

"Your *pyllora . . .*"

"My guide. My counselor. You will help me reconstruct the memory in its entirety. And as I am reliving it, you will help me to objectify my experience. By processing the experience rather than avoiding it," he went on, taking his refuge in the scientific steps, "I can begin to overcome my fear, anger, and other emotional responses. And then I shall try to reintegrate the memory into my conscious mind. Only then will I be free of the destructive emotions associated with the memory."

Sounded simple when he said it like that. She knew there were myriad complications, but the most twisted maze started with the first step, and she was anxious to get going on this most bizarre journey.

"When I'm in your memory," she asked, "will I actually be reliving it with you?"

"No. I will be the only one who will notice your presence. Because these are my memories, it will be easy for me to simply relive the experience instead of analyzing it. I will need you to help guide me through my memories and help me locate the one that has been forgotten. You will be an observer in the memory, not a participant. This will give you the freedom to guide me in an objective manner."

"And when we find the memory?"

"That is a more difficult question to answer," he said. "I do not know what to expect, or how I will respond."

Janeway wondered how formidable a struggle this would be—suspicious because everything so far sounded rather simple. In fact, it didn't sound like anything Tuvok couldn't do for himself. Go into the memory, walk through it, follow all the threads that looked like a little girl tumbling over a cliff, and track her down like lines on a chart. Connect the mental dots.

Still . . .

"When do we start?" she asked.

Right now. Before I have a chance to change my mind.

"I will need time to prepare," Tuvok said. "Please return in one hour."

Damn.

"I wanted to get started right away, but Tuvok needed time. So I'm taking this chance to inform you of our intentions."

"I don't like this, Captain. Why can't one of the other Vulcans do this for him?"

Janeway leaned back in her office chair and looked up at Chakotay. A band of soft lighting behind her caught the lines of the patterned tattoo on the left side of his forehead.

"I can't turn down a chance to help a member of my crew because we're not the same genetic structure," she told him. "What kind of message would that be to the rest of the crew?"

He pressed his lips tight and frowned, thinking about what she had just said. After a moment he paced to the corner of her desk, paused, gazed at the carpet, then looked at her.

"That's true," he allowed, "but you're the captain, for all of us. That also means you shouldn't risk yourself unnecessarily for one crewmember when there's a viable alternative. What kind of message is that? You risk your life—in this case, your mental stability. If you live through the stress of a Vulcan mind-meld of this intensity, you might still come out of it severely brain-damaged. That leaves us without a captain."

Janeway tipped her head. "I believe I would be

63

leaving the crew with a capable captain, or I wouldn't try this."

He didn't fall for it. "Well, that's very flattering, and I appreciate the faith, but I'd like to go down in formal protest to your doing this. Risking you is risking the whole crew. If not physically, then certainly their morale. You are the focal point of all our hopes. You're the one who forged a single crew from Starfleet and Maquis personnel."

He was a single-minded man with many Vulcan-like qualities. If he weren't standing here pointing this out, Tuvok would be the one pointing it out. Janeway knew this was Chakotay's duty as first officer, to help her question anything he believed she had failed to question, but she also knew, from the flint in his eyes, that he believed she was putting herself in danger and that he didn't like that a bit.

Feeling fortunate to have a first officer who wasn't vying in the privacy of his ambitions for an extra pip on his collar and a rank acquired by loss of a commanding officer, Janeway let him have his say.

When he paused, she started to say something, but Chakotay leaned forward on the desk.

"This is just *not* necessary when there are Vulcans on board who can handle the mental and psychological stress better than any human."

"I think you underestimate me," Janeway commented with a little grin.

"I don't underestimate you at all," he claimed. "I just suggest that you accept the limitations of being human."

"I don't consider myself limited because I'm human, Chakotay."

The first officer let his head hang, and gave it a shake. When he looked up again, there was a tug of amusement pulling at his lips. "Are you doing that on purpose, Captain?"

"Doing what on purpose?"

"Twisting my meaning."

"You bet I am."

He shook his head again and pushed himself straight. "Then I don't know what to say."

"You've said it," she consoled. "I understand your concern, and I appreciate your loyalty. I think you're underestimating yourself, actually, but we can have that discussion some other time."

The captain stood up and strode around to the front of her desk, to deplete that sense of captain-subordinate that prevailed when she sat back there and struck out from heaven.

"Commanding *Voyager,*" she began, "in the strange dilemma we're having to live with daily. It's not a matter of looking out for the crew's well-being or making sure nothing happens to myself. We're facing challenges and enemies that no one in the Federation ever had to face before. No Federation starship has ever been so far from home space. Most starships expect to face the unknown, but not *every* single day."

Leaning back on her desk, she hitched a thigh up there and tried to appear comfortable with the idea of what she was planning, so he would feel comfortable too.

"A crocodile is hunting one of us," she said. "It's just below the surface, and we can't see it if we don't put our heads into the water and look around down there. It could be any of us, but we should consider ourselves fortunate that it's Tuvok and there's a way inside. Right now the croc has the advantage, and I mean to take possession of that. Part of being the captain of this particular crew, on this ship in this quadrant, is being willing to go identify my enemy and being willing to go wherever I have to go in order to face it down. Whether the threat is to one crewmember or all of us, this *is* my job. Even if Tuvok weren't my trusted confidant and someone I consider my friend, it's still my job. I've got a running fix on my enemy, and this is the only way I can fight it. If I end up disabled and have to string beads in the infirmary for the rest of the voyage, well . . . just do me a favor."

That half-grin pulled at Chakotay's lips again, because he knew he'd been beaten. "Anything, Captain."

"Knit me a bib, will you? I'd hate to drool on my uniform."

CHAPTER
7

STRANGE WAY TO BEGIN A MISSION. SEATED, FACE-TO-face as if they were about to play patty-cake.

Janeway tried to breathe deeply and evenly as she looked at Tuvok. Around them, the Doctor and Kes were preparing monitors that displayed two diagrams, two separate brain patterns. For a few moments Janeway couldn't control a childish fascination with her own brain pattern.

Like looking inside a bad cut before it's mended . . .

And looking inside somebody else's—Tuvok's brain patterns were completely different from hers. For the first time she wondered if perhaps Chakotay weren't a little bit right. She was venturing into utterly alien territory, alien from her species, alien from her culture. Had she pretended to know Tuvok well enough to pull this off? Was she doing him a favor of devotion or subjecting him to inadequate help?

The Doctor came over to them, said nothing, but fitted a fresh neural device to Tuvok's head, then fitted one to Janeway's. She heard its faint buzz against her skull, even fainter than a nerve twitch. She'd crossed a line now. If she backed out, she'd have to tell them to take the thing off, and that would be tantamount to abandonment of Tuvok. The simple gesture alone would stick with her for the rest of her life, and she'd know she had let him slip over the cliff.

No, she'd stick to her plan and hope Chakotay knew how to knit.

"We're ready when you are, Captain," the Doctor said.

Suddenly embarrassed that she had to be prodded, Janeway nodded to Tuvok.

He had evidently been waiting for that.

Now he lifted his hands slowly. He stopped blinking at all, rapt in concentration. His hands were like sculptures as they spread to the shape of Janeway's face and touched her skin.

Her eyes drifted closed, and she was gazing at the darkness behind her eyelids, aware of the angle of lighting in the sickbay that came through as a faint glow.

The glow began to fade, her mind to blur. Thoughts began blending gently, like tidal waters washing in, out.

Tuvok's voice was scarcely above a whisper. The words sifted through the filaments of both their minds.

"Your mind to my mind . . . your thoughts to my thoughts . . . I am taking us back . . . back to the boy that I was . . . the boy lying on the precipice . . ."

Was this all there was to it?

Janeway's mind began to clear after just a brief swim. She opened her eyes, wondering what had gone wrong with the meld—

And a hard force struck the ship, rocking it violently to the port and shoving the bow slightly downward.

She flailed for balance and reached out to catch Tuvok in case he was still lost in the trance.

He wasn't there.

Fooom.

Another hard jolt. That was no gas cloud! The ship was under attack!

"Tuvok—"

She spoke the word, but there was little sound. The smell of electrical smoke choked her and made her clamp her lips tight until it faded off, dragged away by the whirring vents in the bridge ceiling.

The bridge?

Yes, a starship's bridge. But not *Voyager*'s. In fact, this wasn't any bridge she recognized in Starfleet. This was compact, powerful, tightly arranged, with a distinct central design.

And it certainly wasn't a Vulcan plateau with a child hanging over the cliff's edge. Where in hell was she?

All around her, consoles crackled and sparked, and people who were clearly Starfleet dashed through screens of smoke and flashing destruction. Space battle.

Old-style uniforms. Sixty or seventy years ago, if she recalled correctly.

What was Tuvok doing?

She flinched as an ensign dodged past her so close that she smelled the electrical burns on his sleeve. He hadn't noticed her, or acknowledged that he had nearly run her down.

Astonishing! She had expected to "see" events like something on a viewscreen, but this was even more real than a holoprogram. She felt the air and the vibrations of the ship. How real was this? Could she actually be injured if she *believed* she was? Could she be killed in action here, even in her mind, and have her body be affected?

Was she really here? Or still sitting back in sickbay?

She had to be still there, back on *Voyager,* seventy high-warp years in the wrong direction from the place she saw around her, but she *felt* here . . .

She raised her hand and rubbed her fingers together. Yup, same old fingers. Wherever she was, her hands and toes were here, too.

Starfleet ship, full-sized exploratory vessel. She glanced around to get a hint of the design style and ship's nomenclature. It was here somewhere. All ships had their identification name, registry number, and date of launch somewhere on the bridge.

She looked aft, past the engineering station—no, that was communications on this design. Back near the turbolift doors was a dedication plaque.

U.S.S. Excelsior, Starfleet Registry NCC-2000. Commissioned: Stardate 8105.5

That was decades ago.

"Damage report!"

At the sound of the deep, rough voice in a tone she recognized intimately, Janeway turned toward the darkest part of the bridge, where a purple-black gusher of smoke piled from the deck housing.

A man stepped forward out of the boiling veil, a lean Asian man with sharp features, pitch-black hair, and an officer's maroon uniform jacket. A captain.

Captain Hikaru Sulu!

PART TWO

PART
TWO

"Better to die on our feet than live on our knees."

Brigadier Kerla
Klingon High Command
Star Trek VI: The Undiscovered Country

CHAPTER

8

ACTION ROILED ACROSS THE BRIDGE. PEOPLE PLUNGED back and forth, trying to stabilize the consoles and keep energy and information flowing. Janeway recognized the whole drill.

From one quick glance around, she knew they were under attack by other vessels, but didn't see any subsystems monitor displaying enemy ships. Some monitors were blacked out, and that might've been their job. Maybe part of the ship's sensing system had been knocked for a loop.

Captain Sulu never got his damage report, and after a moment gave up and took over two of the consoles himself. There was still someone at the helm, so Sulu stayed on the upper bridge, trying to hold the ship together. Thrum after thrum of firing impact sounded against the vessel's shields, sending the orientation grids spinning—which meant the ship was spinning.

"Hull breach on deck twelve," a female lieutenant commander reported finally from a console. "Section forty-seven . . . we've lost power on decks five, six, and ten . . . casualty reports are coming in . . . nineteen wounded . . ."

"Helm, drop out of warp," Captain Sulu interrupted. "Evasive pattern Delta Six."

What a voice! Janeway had studied about the legendary captain of the first *Excelsior*-class vessel, but had never heard a recording of his voice. He didn't seem excited, and in fact was only speaking loudly enough to be heard above the crackle and boom of battle. He didn't have to speak very loudly to be heard, with that heavy voice to throw around.

Now, where was Tuvok?

She took a step forward on the upper deck, since these people didn't seem to see her anyway.

She was overwhelmed with a desire to plunge in and help, to give orders. That crewman over there should be on the other side of the bridge, stabilizing the shield grid. What was he waiting for?

Didn't they have backup compensators?

No, maybe back then—back now—they didn't.

And there was Hikaru Sulu, a living history lesson. If only she could pin herself to his sleeve and question his every decision.

No—there was something to be accomplished here, and it didn't involve a captain from eighty years ago. It involved Tuvok. Where was he?

She looked around.

Knee-high smoke curled toward the deck vents, gradually clearing the navigation area on the lower deck. There, in the hub of the bridge, normally the most precious place on the ship, Tuvok sat on the deck, dressed in the same kind of old-style uniform as everyone else here, with an ensign's insignia and the designation of a science officer. In his arms was a human shipmate, a young man wearing the same kind of uniform, with lieutenant's insignia. The young officer was badly burned, blood oozing through gory wounds on his face and hands.

Janeway recognized the type of injury. Close-ignition electrical burns from an exploded circuit board. The small gray-blue dots of hot console insulation pocking the young man's burned face were the giveaway. They'd been fused right into his skin, then incinerated into place.

All around them battle dialogue shot back and forth across the bridge. She knew what was going on, but not why. They were firing phasers, and the ship continued to shake and rock and bolt. Captain Sulu was snapping off orders one after another, and answering questions while also handling a couple of consoles. It took all Janeway's self-control to ignore the situation and concentrate on her purpose for being here.

"Tuvok," she began, flinching at the sound of her own voice, "can you hear me?"

Tuvok looked up, startled at first, then eased his crewmate's body to the ground. He stood up, and seemed confused.

"Yes," he said. "It would seem that the meld was successful."

Janeway let out a breath she'd been holding. She was relieved—he did see her.

He didn't really look younger, but of course he didn't look a hundred years old, either. For a moment she was jealous of Vulcan longevity. Imagine what humans could accomplish if they lived a lifetime and a half the way Vulcans did. What any human wouldn't give to age so gracefully!

"We are not in a childhood memory," Tuvok said.

"Where are we?" she asked. She knew the place and time, but wanted to hear him say it, to keep his mind concentrating on the reason they were here, the reason he had to feel a crewmate die in his arms all over again.

"This event *is* a memory of mine," he said. "But it is my first deep-space assignment . . . aboard the *Excelsior.*"

Vulcan or not, there was a touch of awe and amazement at the detail of this vision all around them. To actually step back in time and relive a key moment—even he couldn't keep the emotion out of his voice.

No matter how accurate, stimulating, or fun, this memory was the wrong one.

"Why did you bring us here?" Janeway asked.

"I did not intend to."

"Can you take us to the precipice?" She tried to keep focus in spite of her own fascination. "To the girl?"

"That is precisely what I attempted to do," he said, perplexed.

She moved through the smoke to his side. "The memory is within you. Focus on it. Take us to the girl."

He paused, held still a moment, closed his eyes, then opened them and looked around again.

"It is no use, Captain. I cannot."

The ship vibrated fiercely under impact of disruptor fire, and Janeway fought the elevator-drop feeling until the ship compensated under her. Well, that was certainly real enough!

The ship's crew dashed around them, without noticing her. However, they did step over the dead lieutenant's body and obviously veer to miss hitting Tuvok.

So they saw *him,* at least.

She watched the activity for a moment, and couldn't help hoping the ship survived and the crew made it all right. Of course, she knew they had made it. Still . . .

"There must be some reason your mind brought us here," she pursued. "Maybe *this* memory is connected to the girl in some way. Were there any children on this ship?"

"No. It was a standard Starfleet crew. No families."

"Were there any similar incidents on board? Did anyone close to you die?"

Tuvok turned, and looked down at the body of the young lieutenant, whose blood and skin fragments still clung to Tuvok's hands and clothing. "Lieutenant Dimitri Valtane was killed in a plasma blast . . . he was my cabin mate."

I'd call that a big yes, Janeway thought, but kept it to herself. This was a long way from a little girl on a Vulcan plateau, though.

"Do you sense a connection with the girl?" she persisted. "Similar feelings of anxiety? Fear?"

He looked at the dead crewman and tried to concentrate, but there was no hope in his expression. After a moment he said, "No, I do not."

"There must be some reason your mind brought us here," Janeway insisted. "How long ago is this?"

"Stardate nine-five-two-one. Approximately eighty years ago."

"Who are you fighting?"

"The Klingons."

Janeway grasped his arm. "Klingons! Before you passed out in engineering, you thought we were approaching Klingon space. Remember?"

"Yes . . ."

Another shake tore through the ship, and Captain Sulu had to clasp the console he was operating to keep from being thrown sideways. He looked up, seemed to look right through Janeway at the upper subsystems screens, then looked down again.

"Let's stay with this memory for now," Janeway suggested. "See if we can find any more commonalities. Any psychological connections to the death of the girl. Tuvok, *why* are you fighting the Klingons?"

He thought for a moment, sifting through myriad instances in his memory from which his mind had to choose.

"This battle began with an incident that took place three days before."

"Can you take us there?"

"Captain, this is not simply a shuttle ride in which I program the navigational computer."

"I understand that," she said, experiencing her first touch of impatience with him. "I'm doing my assignment. Yours is to let me suggest the pattern of focus. Try to focus on what happened three days ago. There's some connection here, and I'm going to find it. Concentrate. Three days ago . . . where were you?"

She glanced around the battered bridge, then looked again to her side, but Tuvok was gone.

Then the bridge also was gone, and she was blinking into bright, shadowless artificial lighting. Strange that her eyes had needed to adjust to different fragments of memory. Strange indeed how very physically real all this seemed. The floor she was standing on, the scent of the starship air, the aroma of tea . . . particularly herbal with a touch of some exotic spices. Maybe a fruit or two.

She looked toward the tea.

Tuvok stood, clean as a whistle and fresh as a morning shower, over a hotplate on which he was feeding herbs into a teapot. A row of bunks lined one wall.

Junior officers' sleeping quarters.

So what was a lieutenant doing hanging around here—suddenly Janeway recognized the lieutenant.

A moment ago he had been lying crusty and smoldering on the deck of the bridge.

Valtane—alive!

There were two other junior officers moving about here too, polishing their boots, chatting casually, doing routine chores.

For a moment Janeway lost herself in the secure scene and wished for a moment to be a junior officer again, to have other people making the life-or-death decisions. This was one of the most heavily shielded bunkers on a starship, and she felt particularly safe here.

How long had it been since she'd even visited the J.O. quarters on board *Voyager?*

Janeway moved quickly to Tuvok's side. "Give me a quick summary of this ship's mission history."

Tuvok didn't raise his eyes, and kept his voice low. "Captain Sulu has been in command of *Excelsior* for three years. Valtane is a xenogeologist," he added, glancing at the other young man. "Relations between the Federation and the Klingons are presently strained, after the Kudao massacre—"

"I don't want that much detail. Just the overview."

"Very well. The ship's current assignment is to conduct scientific research near the Klingon Neutral Zone and provide a strong presence in the Beta Quadrant. Tension is high. One more attack from either side will result in confrontation."

"But that didn't happen," Janeway pointed out, vowing to keep Tuvok from slipping too deeply into this illusion.

"To mask the military purpose of our being here, we involved ourselves in scientific analysis and mapping—"

"All right, gamma shift! It's time to defend the Federation against gaseous anomalies!"

Janeway spun to see a clean-cut blond female lieutenant commander stride in the entrance. She looked like . . . yes, she was the same officer who had also been on the bridge. Could she be the connection?

The young officers dropped what they were doing, jumped to attention, and began to file out the door.

"Gaseous anomalies," she repeated, keeping her voice down by reflex. "We were charting a gaseous anomaly on *Voyager.*"

Tuvok hurried to finish the tea he was brewing. "And that is when my problems began," he murmured. He evidently had a real reason to keep his voice down, since these people could hear him.

"That's more than a coincidence," Janeway uttered. "Who's the woman?"

"Commander Janice Rand. Communications. Long career. She is nearing retirement and very happy about that, as I recall. She has an easygoing manner and has taken a particular interest in—"

He stopped as Rand vectored and came around to him and the teapot he was feeding.

"How are you this morning, Ensign?" the woman asked.

"I am well, Commander," Tuvok answered. "Thank you."

"I thought you might like to see some of this morning's comm traffic before you go on duty."

She handed him a PADD.

"There's a message from the *Yorktown* that I thought you might be interested in," she added. "It's from your parents."

As he continued to stir his tea, Tuvok eyed the PADD. "Thank you."

Rand grinned and nodded at the tea. "You're not going to have time to drink that, you know. You're due on the bridge in five minutes."

"It is not for me," he told her. "It is for the captain. I have observed that Captain Sulu drinks a cup of tea each morning. I thought he might enjoy a Vulcan blend."

"Oh, I see." Rand's grin widened into a smile, and she eyed him cagily. "Trying to make lieutenant in your first month? I wish I'd thought of that when I was your age. It took me three years just to make ensign."

Janeway grinned, too, when Tuvok seemed suddenly desperate to be understood correctly.

"I assure you," he insisted with a tinge of protest, "I have no ulterior motive."

Rand narrowed her gaze and nodded disbelievingly. "Whatever you say, Ensign. See you on the bridge."

She headed out.

Tuvok picked up the pot of tea as if he didn't realize that Janeway was still there. The memory was pulling him away from the reality, because, for him, this was the reality of the moment.

He picked up his teapot and headed for the door.
Janeway fell in beside him and matched his pace.

"You never brought *me* tea," she pointed out
lightly, eyeing him in much the same way Janice
Rand had.

He glanced at her, almost flinching as if he were
surprised to see her, then relaxing as if realizing who
she was.

"You prefer coffee," he mentioned. "And Vulcan
coffee would paralyze your nervous system and
atrophy your pancreas. But I will make you some, if
you wish."

A strange, surreal place. Surreal, only because this
in fact *was* real. Or had been real once.

Venturing into the past in any case was somehow
unnatural, no matter how fascinating. Janeway was
aware of her mind playing tricks on her, beginning to
believe this was happening around her. She was
hovering in the shadows of the bridge, even though
she knew these people couldn't see her, even though
she knew they weren't really people at all, but only
phantoms.

Yet she could more than see them. She sensed, felt,
believed their presence, could smell the odors of the
bridge . . . the carpet, the freshly painted bulkheads.
How could a memory have scent?

And the scent of tea, too.

Tuvok was just handing the brew to his captain.

Captain Sulu was supremely Vulcan in his
manner—very subdued, unflappable, with that glint

of underlying amusement Janeway had seen in some Vulcans.

Not Tuvok, but some.

"Outstanding," Captain Sulu said after sipping the tea. "I may have to give you a promotion."

From one of the bridge stations, Commander Rand smiled, and that little bit of attention made Tuvok stiffen with self-consciousness.

"That was not my motivation, Captain," he said, irritated at being misinterpreted. "I am not attempting to curry favor with you in any way."

"Mr. Tuvok," Sulu said with a tiny curve at the corner of his lips, "if you're going to remain on my ship, you're going to have to learn how to appreciate a joke. And don't tell me Vulcans don't have a sense of humor . . . because I know better."

"I will . . . work on it, sir."

"Very good. And thanks again."

Janeway controlled her own grin in case Tuvok glanced at her, but she couldn't help being pleased at the common train of thought between herself and this echo of early Starfleet leadership. Then she remembered—Captain Sulu had served his longest post aboard the *Enterprise,* under Captain James T. Kirk and First Officer Spock. Spock, the first Vulcan to enter Starfleet, the prototype for many who came after. His had been the most true battle of personal will, trying to find a place for the stern, deep-laden control of emotions among a crew of suspicious and uneased humans who were constantly coaxing those emotions out. Spock's will and method had been severely tested, sometimes cruelly shredded, and ultimately molded into a whole new kind of Vulcan. Most Vulcans before him had stayed on their own planet or served aboard ships manned solely by other Vulcans. Tuvok, so much less malleable than many, even than many Vulcans, could never function in a human crew if the tolerance of humans and others hadn't been tempered by those such as Spock and the early Starfleet crews with whom he served.

Sulu took another sip of tea, and Tuvok retreated to his science station in the forward portion of the bridge, near the main viewer. Janeway glanced about self-consciously, then followed him and stepped to his side.

She glanced back at Sulu, absorbing the way unforgiving bridge lighting creased his Asian features and made his black hair look like a helmet.

"He doesn't look anything like his portrait at Starfleet Headquarters," she mentioned.

"In the twenty-third century," Tuvok said, "holographic imaging resolution was less accurate."

Janeway looked at him. That was a pretty terse answer for a subjective comment. He was disturbed by all this, fiercely avoiding any thread of attachment. This must be very hard for him, she guessed.

"This is a science station, isn't it?" she asked, cooperating with his demeanor.

"Yes," he said. "I am one of several junior science officers."

He sat down and started pecking at the controls.

"Tuvok," Janeway persisted, "why doesn't your

service record reflect any of this? I thought your first assignment was aboard the *Wyoming.*"

His jaw tightened, and he frowned but didn't look up. "It is a . . . long story. Suffice it to say this was my *first* Starfleet career. I was twenty-nine years old."

First Starfleet career? What was that supposed to mean? Was he a *dentist* in between?

All right, he didn't want to talk about it. So she'd file it away with all the other stories she was determined to get out of him someday, and she went on.

"So what's happening? Are we about to encounter the Klingons?"

"Not exactly." Tuvok kept his voice low, and gazed at his monitor as if seeing into a crystal ball. "The Klingon moon Praxis is about to explode."

"Praxis . . ."

"During this period, it was the primary source of energy for the Klingon homeworld."

"Praxis," Janeway repeated, as if chanting. "Yes. Its destruction would have lasting repercussions throughout the quadrant. And it led to the first Federation-Klingon peace treaty."

"That is correct."

Yes, of course it was correct. Janeway noted Tuvok's discomfort again. He wasn't just confirming, but stating the incredibly obvious. He was trying to help, but they weren't getting anywhere.

Praxis. Janeway scoured her memory. History had never been her academic strength, exactly. Overmining, bad safety standards—a reactor exploded, a massive chain reaction that rocked the homeworld and contaminated the atmosphere. Violent weather changes nearly decimated agriculture over the long term, on top of a big loss in energy production and dilithium, which everybody and his mother needed for space travel at hyperlight speeds. The Klingons started lobbying for a treaty with the Federation. For the first time in their long and rocky history, the spiteful, aggressive Klingons had to admit that they just plain needed help. They simply couldn't afford to remain hostile.

So the Federation had sent—aha! another link— Captain Kirk and the *Enterprise* to reach out to the Klingon chancellor as a symbolic gesture.

But what were the years? Sulu wasn't on board the *Enterprise* by then. Was "then" . . . now? Right now?

Janeway glanced around, troubled. "But what does all this have to do with the girl on the precipice?"

She started to say something else, but instinct overruled her thought. A faint vibration through the carpet under her feet—very faint, but distinctive. Not the kind of vibration a ship makes from its own power sources.

She stiffened her legs and paused, trying to read the hieroglyphics of experience and instinct.

Suddenly the vibration became stronger, and visible. The whole ship started shaking, as if attached to an automatic sifter. The captain's teacup clattered on its saucer and began a skittering walk across his tabletop.

The captain and crew looked around—nobody else knew what was happening, either. What could make a starship tremble?

The teacup skittered, dumped over the table's edge, and shattered on the deck, but Captain Sulu wasn't paying attention to it anymore, not even to the scalding tea that splashed across his forearm. Now the vibration was so violent that everything around Janeway had a visual blur.

From another science console, Dimitri Valtane shouted, "I have an energy wave from two-four-zero mark six port—"

Sulu stood up. "Visual."

The bridge was abruptly washed with ghastly lights as a wave of superheated gas and inflamed debris flushed toward them out of deep space, as if someone with a flamethrower had made a wide arc. There wasn't any end to it that Janeway could see, but only a burning silvery disk of pure energy rioting toward the ship.

"Shields—" She gasped.

"My God!" Sulu reacted. "Shields! *Shields!*"

Had anyone heard him over the red alert klaxon? Janeway hoped so—she didn't know the end to this story. She knew *Excelsior* hadn't been destroyed, but what cost had there been to salvation? What would the damage be? How many crew lost?

The ship was struck then by the wave, and heeled up viciously as if gut-punched, lurching to starboard. Captain Sulu braced himself on his chair, but stayed upright. Beside Janeway, Tuvok grasped for the soft rim of the science console. Janeway felt the lurch, but she managed to stay balanced, perhaps because she believed what she saw even more than all these people did.

Before she could pat herself on the back, another hand of force rocked the ship and dropped the deck out from under her. She and Tuvok both went tumbling in the same direction. The noise was hideous—a scratching, whining shriek that wouldn't quit.

The bridge crew looked as if a scarecrow had exploded. Hands, legs, tumbling everywhere—oh, yes, still attached to confused and banged-up bodies. Sulu reached down and helped Valtane back onto his feet, but the captain was apparently waiting for the ship and crew to recover before he started barking orders. Pretty restrained. Not bad.

"What the hell is going on?" was all he said, and not to anyone in particular.

The energy wave was still flushing past them, creating a constant, uneven buffeting, but the crew was crawling back to position and digging for answers. At the helm a Halkan crewman gasped, "Captain, helm is not answering!"

"Starboard thrusters!" Sulu ordered. "Turn her into the wave!"

"Under Article 184 of your Interstellar Law, I'm placing you under arrest. You are charged with assassinating the Chancellor of the High Council."

Klingon General Chang,
charging Captain James T. Kirk
and Dr. Leonard H. McCoy with the
murder of Chancellor Gorkon

CHAPTER
9

YES—THAT MIGHT WORK. THRUSTERS WERE INDEPEN-
dent of main steering power and would still be
operational. Well, maybe.

"Aye!" The helmsman said, gulping.

The energy wave on the forward screen was changing color every few seconds as Janeway pushed
herself up to look at it. Coolant leaks hissed and spat
all around the bridge now, distorting a call from the
lower decks.

*"Captain Sulu, engine room! What's going on
up—"*

"Quarter impulse power!" Sulu called.

The Halkan struggled with his controls, but the
cumbersome saucer section of the ship nosed around
to starboard and took the energy flush head-on. That
would put all the ship's aerodynamic design charac-

teristics into play to stabilize her despite the pummeling, and provide a narrowed profile in the face of the destructive energy.

The wave pulsed onward for many seconds, long seconds. Janeway ached to do something, to participate, ask questions, give orders—

But before she could think of any, the wave flushed past, and finally the last rocky bits of debris pounded across the ship like pebbles skipping on water, and it was all over.

"Damage report," Sulu requested as he crawled back into his command chair and squared off.

"Checking all systems, Captain," somebody responded.

"Don't tell me that was any meteor shower," Sulu said, eyeing a shocked and numb Valtane.

"Negative," Valtane managed after a swallow. He licked his lips and drew a breath. "The subspace shock wave originated at bearing three-two-three mark seven-five . . . location . . ."

"Praxis," Janeway murmured, her hands cold.

"It's Praxis, sir," Valtane said. "It's a Klingon moon."

Sulu scowled. "Praxis is their key energy-producing facility!" He twisted around to his communications station, where Commander Rand was sitting. "Send to Klingon High Command—'This is *U.S.S. Excelsior,* a Federation starship traveling through the Beta Quadrant. We have monitored a large explosion in your sector. Do you require assistance?'"

As she responded, he ignored her and turned back to Valtane. "Mr. Valtane, any more data?"

"I've confirmed the location, sir, but . . ."

"What is it?"

"I can't confirm the existence of Praxis. My scanners are focused on the Amrite solar system, on the correct coordinates." He stopped talking as Sulu hurried to the station and looked at the sensor readouts for himself. Even from here Janeway could see the glitter of dead rock and chips that was hardly enough to make up a moon of any notable mass.

"Praxis?" Sulu uttered.

"What's left of it, sir," Valtane murmured significantly.

Janeway moved back to Tuvok's side. "So what happened?" she asked. "Did you go to Praxis?"

As if there was anything left to *go* to—

"No. We were warned off by the Klingons," Tuvok explained quietly. "We resumed our survey mission. However, two days later, we learned that two Starfleet officers had been accused of murdering the Klingon chancellor. They were brought to the Klingon homeworld to stand trial."

"Can we go to two days later?"

"I shall attempt such a transfer . . ."

Janeway held her breath and waited. *Then why can't we transfer to the cliff and the little girl?*

"It is the judgment of this court, that without possibility of reprieve or parole, you'll be taken from this place to the dilithium mines on the

penal asteroid of Rura Penthe, there to spend
the rest of your natural lives."

The sentence of Kirk and McCoy

There was hardly any change. Janeway thought for
a moment that Tuvok had failed, until she realized
that much of the deck damage had now been cleaned
up, and the junior officers milling about the bridge
were different people from an instant ago.

Captain Sulu was still here, Valtane, Rand,
Tuvok—but now everyone was tense, glowering.
Voices were low. Sulu was pacing.

Janeway and Tuvok watched the captain for a
moment.

"Captain Sulu had served under both Captain
Kirk and Dr. Leonard McCoy for many years. And
he felt an intense loyalty to both of them," Tuvok
said.

"As I recall," Janeway said, "they were released
from Rura Penthe."

"Yes, they were sentenced and sent there, but they
were innocent. The assassination was engineered by
others, and Kirk and McCoy were implicated. Captain Sulu believed—"

"Captain," Rand spoke up then, "we're receiving
a coded message. It's not on one of the normal
Starfleet channels." She looked at the captain. "It's
from the *Enterprise.*"

Sulu nearly pounced on the message. His reaction
suggested that he'd been waiting for this. "Let's see
it. On screen."

The main viewer wiggled with a shaky, non-regulation-channel picture of a supremely poised black woman with commander's insignia on her uniform.

"Uhura," Sulu said with obvious recognition. "Are you watching the trial?"

"I'm watching the thing they're calling a trial," the woman said. Her voice was deep and eminently schooled.

"So what are you going to do about it?"

"Spock's told Starfleet Command that our warp engines are down," the woman said. "And we've been specifically ordered not to interfere."

Neither of them seemed surprised. It was as if they were communicating in code.

"I can't believe," Sulu said, "you're just going to sit there. We both know how Klingon 'justice' works. They'll end up in prison for the rest of their lives, or worse."

The elegant woman raised a practiced eyebrow. "We have our orders, Hikaru."

Janeway peered suspiciously at them both. There was more going on than either was saying. They were communicating on a subliminal level, as people did who knew each other for decades, who worked too closely for description, through events no one really liked to describe.

"How's your survey mission going?" Uhura asked, but that wasn't what she was really talking about.

"It's nearly complete," Sulu answered.

And he meant something else too.

"You know," the woman went on, "there are rather interesting gaseous anomalies in the Klingon Empire."

"So I hear . . ."

"Well . . . good luck with your survey."

"Thanks," Sulu said. "Good luck with your warp engines."

Uhura winked without really winking. Somehow she did it with her voice. "Scotty's working on them right now. I have a feeling they'll be up and running before you know it." She smiled—a lot more of a smile than anyone would whose captain and ship's surgeon were condemned to a lethal rock like Rura Penthe. *"Enterprise* out."

The image blurred to stars. Sulu smiled and returned to his command chair.

"Helm," he said once he got settled, "set a course for Kronos maximum warp. Take us through the Azure Nebula. That should conceal our approach."

"Aye, aye, sir," the helmsman said, and suddenly everything on the bridge seemed to take a long, steadying breath. People moved a little faster, and some even smiled. They leaned into their controls and hungered for what was before them.

Janeway recognized that.

"I don't get it," she murmured. "What's going on?"

"He is about to attempt a rescue of Captain Kirk and Dr. McCoy. As you can see," Tuvok added, displeased, "everyone seemed perfectly willing to go along with this breach of orders. However, I felt differently."

As if there were no difference between his reality and his memory, Tuvok turned and stepped toward Captain Sulu. Was he reliving the moment, or was he lost in it?

Janeway almost reached out to stop him, to remind him that this was a meld-induced incident.

Yet, as if some other unseen hand instead took her arm, she paused and let the moment play out.

"Captain," Tuvok began, "am I correct in assuming you have decided to embark on a rescue mission?"

Sulu blinked at him in a detached manner. "That's right," his deep voice rumbled. "Do you have a problem with that, Ensign?"

Tuvok visibly isolated himself from whatever loyalties were driving Sulu. "I do," he said, now that he was committed. "It is a direct violation of our orders from Starfleet Command. And it could precipitate an armed conflict between the Klingon Empire and the Federation."

Sulu tipped his shoulders casually, unimpressed by the rote rhetoric. "Objection noted. Resume your post."

"Sir . . . as a Starfleet officer," Tuvok pushed on, "it is my duty to formally protest."

The bridge changed—everyone turned to look in unmasked astonishment at their fellow crewman.

From communications, Commander Rand barely parted her lips to warn, "Tuvok . . ."

Captain Sulu eyed him sedately, and under the

pastel amusement was a definite line of demarcation. "A pretty bold statement for an ensign with less than two months' space duty under his belt."

"I am aware of my limited experience," Tuvok agreed, and there was definitely a tightness of discomfort under his protest. "However, I am also very much aware of Starfleet regulations . . . and my obligation to carry them out."

Janice Rand stood up instantly. "That's enough," she snapped. "Ensign, you're relieved." Turning to Sulu, she added, "I'm sorry about this, Captain. I assure you it won't happen again."

But Sulu raised a hand to stop her, and to rivet Tuvok to his place there.

"Ensign," he said slowly, "you're absolutely right. But you're also absolutely wrong. You'll find that more happens on the bridge of a starship than just carrying out orders and observing regulations. There's a sense of loyalty to the men and women you serve with, a sense of family. Those two men on trial . . . I served with them for a long time. I owe them my life a dozen times over. And right now, they're in trouble. And I'm going to help them." A certain onyx glint rose in Sulu's eyes as he finished: "Let the regulations be damned."

Janeway found her throat tight with empathy. As a starship's captain she knew that the command chair meant endless lines to be drawn and lines to be crossed. The senior position on a starship, a ship of such fabulous constructive and destructive power that the galaxy bowed before it, meant continually drawing one's own lines while daring to cross lines drawn by others. A series of dares and counterdares that never seemed to end, until one day the odds increased too far in somebody else's direction. There weren't all that many starship captains over the generations who managed to stay alive long enough to retire in dignity.

Maybe this was one of the reasons Captain James Kirk stayed alive long enough to retire with honors. Maybe Captain Sulu stuck his neck out in answer to all those times Kirk had done the sticking and the risking.

Would anybody do that for me? she wondered.

As the unbidden thought roiled in her mind, Tuvok started talking again, pushing his luck.

"Sir," the young Vulcan went on, "that is a most illogical line of reasoning."

Sulu shifted in his chair with a dismissive manner. "You'd better believe it. Helm, engage."

The bridge crew collectively turned away from Tuvok, canceling out his protest, his presence, his potency. He was left standing alone, embarrassed, in the middle of the bridge. No one would look at him.

Slowly he turned and came back to his console. Was the embarrassment attached to the moment, or to the memory? Was Janeway looking at reality or regret? Would Tuvok do it again if he had a second chance?

A *real* second chance?

Janeway met him at his post.

"You know," she said, feeling obliged, "you did the right thing."

Troubled by this unrequested memory, Tuvok murmured a pitiful, "Perhaps."

"Tuvok, help me!"

Staring suddenly, Tuvok sucked a breath and held it.

Beside him, Janeway went numb as her mind was suddenly flooded with dread.

And she heard the cry—

"Tuvok!"

CHAPTER

10

"DOCTOR! IT'S HAPPENING TO HIM AGAIN!"

Kes held her hands out to her sides as if to balance herself, and she stared past the Doctor to the shivering body of Mr. Tuvok, still locked in the mind-meld with the captain.

"Kes?" The Doctor hurried to her. "Are you involved? Do you feel as if you're integrating into the vision again?"

"I can see some of it . . . but there's someone else there now. It's the captain . . . I can see the captain . . . on the plateau . . . something's happening to Tuvok . . . we have to help him! We have to help him!"

She shoved past the Doctor and plunged toward Tuvok and the captain, but the Doctor caught her. "No!" he said sharply. "Don't touch them! Don't!

We have to do this with medication. Kes, do you understand?"

He shook her rather harshly, until the pain of his grip distracted her from what was happening in the recesses of her mind, and she drew back from the captain and the Vulcan.

"Yes . . . I'm sorry. Tell me what to do."

"Fifty milligrams cordrazine!"

Even to people who didn't really know what it was, cordrazine caused a wince of intimidation and fear. Very touchy medication, this. Almost as dangerous as the things it cured.

Kathryn Janeway reached out to help Tuvok hold the girl, to pull her back over the top of the plateau . . .

A child, a Vulcan female child—dangling over a precipice, with a Vulcan boy clasping her desperately with one hand. The other hand was braced on the chipping edge of the plateau. He wasn't strong enough to hold on.

The girl—maybe six or eight years old—had no Vulcan reserve blocking the terror in her face. She was fully aware of what was happening to her, and she was blatantly horrified. If anyone ever believed a child couldn't absorb the full meaning of not being alive anymore, the look in her eyes would shatter that.

Below the rocks were jagged, toothy.

Janeway reached out, but her hand was little more than a fuzzy blur at her hip. She couldn't step forward. This was like one of those dreams where the goal kept getting farther away no matter how much she ran and ran—

When Janeway heard her ship's doctor call for cordrazine, she wasn't sure anymore where she was or what had happened. She saw Tuvok's face before her, glazed and shocky, staring, but not seeing her. His fingertips were on her face, trembling fitfully against her cheeks and temples.

Then his touch fell away, and his face drifted backward. He was falling.

She sat stunned, watching as *Voyager*'s doctor appeared in her periphery.

The meld . . .

Broken.

And Tuvok lay before her, convulsing slightly.

What had broken the meld? The shock of the little girl falling?

In her mind she saw a wash of blue . . . tumbling azure—

"The Azure Nebula," she murmured, barely more than a whisper. Neither the Doctor nor Kes heard her.

"Captain! Captain, are you all right?" the Doctor said sharply, in a tone clearly meant to shake her up. "Captain, come out of it! Are you all right?"

Janeway swallowed and choked out, "Yes . . . yes . . . fine. What happened?"

"Let's get him onto a bio-bed," the Doctor said. "Not you, Captain. I'll do it. You're still stressed. Sit there and give us a chance to examine him. You need to gain back your strength."

Obviously he knew something about how her

mind had reacted that Janeway didn't know. She didn't really care to know. Sense was gradually returning; she knew where she was, and why she was here.

So why were her hands still shuddering?

She still saw the Azure Nebula in her mind—Sulu and the *Excelsior* charging willfully toward the twisting mass of chemical blue. They'd gone right into it.

And that was when Tuvok had lost control over the meld. Why? What was it about that nebula?

She sat alone for several minutes, until the Doctor came to get her. He took her by the elbow and led her aside, while Kes stayed behind to tend Tuvok.

Kes looked very pale and worried as she gazed at Tuvok, her hand reaching out as though to give him a comforting pat, but her fingers only opening and closing fitfully without ever touching him.

"There was a sudden disruption in his hippocampus," the Doctor said. "Luckily, he was in sickbay, or he'd be in a coma right now."

He leaned to one side and checked a monitor, then frowned.

"That's the good news. The bad news is that his synaptic pathways are continuing to degrade. If the repressed memory keeps resurfacing on its own, it's going to cause more and more damage. Eventually, his entire neural structure will collapse," he finished uneasily, "resulting in brain death."

Holograph or not, the Doctor didn't like saying that.

Janeway could barely control the twitch of

concern—fear—on her face as she glanced back at Tuvok. He seemed so uncharacteristically helpless . . .

"We were just starting to make some progress. We finally accessed the repressed memory. I saw Tuvok as a boy. And the girl on the precipice."

The memory disturbed her as if it were her own. She saw again the poor little girl's abject terror, bolting through Tuvok's thoughts into her own, a perception so real and so utter than no one could simply imagine it without having actually seen it at some time or other.

Had it happened? Had Tuvok once clung to a Vulcan girl and let her fall?

But he was only a boy.

"Can I talk to him?" she asked.

"Not yet," the Doctor told her. "He suffered a severe neural trauma, so I'm keeping him sedated for the next few hours. I'll let you know when it's safe to revive him."

Part of her was relieved. The rest—she just wanted to get back in there and get this over with.

She managed her best commandatorial nod, turned, and headed for the door.

Suddenly she stopped and spun around. "I know what it was!"

The Doctor and Kes both looked up. "Pardon me?" the Doctor said.

"I know what set off this episode!"

"Yes?"

"We were on board the *Excelsior,* and we were just approaching the Azure Nebula!"

"Azure . . . you mean—"

"Yes! It was very similar to the sirillium nebula we tracked when all this started! Doctor, could the color blue be a factor? Is that possible?"

"Well," the Doctor began, his animated eyes working, "I am familiar with a few cases in which chromatic stimulus had resulted in epileptic-type reactions or set off abnormal activity. That tendency has been a tried-and-true method of mind control, often used in espionage."

"Doctor, are you making a suggestion?"

"That Mr. Tuvok might be a pawn in some larger scheme? Of course, you will have to make that judgment, barring any physical proof. But I'll run some tests, if you like."

"Yes, do that. A clue is a clue." She tapped her commbadge. "Janeway to Kim."

"Kim here, Captain."

"Ensign, I want you to call up any data we have on the Azure Nebula in the Beta Quadrant and do a full-spectrum comparison with the sirillium anomaly we came through. Report to me in my ready room as soon as you have that. Sooner, if possible."

"Doctor! Doctor, come quickly!"

Neelix struggled into the sickbay with Kes in his arms. She murmured softly and desperately against his shoulder, words he didn't understand, things he had never heard from her before. Every few seconds a shiver went through her from head to foot, all through her bones, and he felt every tremor as he clutched her against him.

The Doctor appeared out of his usual cocoon of empty air and hurried to them just as Neelix put Kes on the diagnostic bed.

"What's wrong with her?" Neelix asked. "What's happening to her? She's saying crazy things I've never heard before. Things about falling and slipping and dying! Doctor, does she need a transfusion? A transplant? I can provide anything she needs! I'll be her donor!"

The Doctor bent over Kes with a bio-scanner. "She doesn't need a transplant or transfusion, and even if she did, you're Talaxian and she's Ocampa, and I seriously doubt any of your organs or fluids would be compatible. It's tricky enough to find compatibility between people of the same species." He paused, then straightened. "However, I did once hear of a successful pancreatic transplant between an African Cape buffalo and an Orion. However, that was very likely—"

"Doctor, please . . . what's wrong with Kes? Is there anything at all *I* can do?"

The Doctor gazed at him, then only said, "Not presently." He bent over Kes again, reading the information clicking through the bio-scanner and the diagnostic panel of the bed.

Plucking a ready hypospray from a sterile table, he spritzed it into the side of Kes's neck.

On the cushion, Kes twitched and moaned, constantly in distressful movement, her head turning back and forth, her eyes partly open, but seeing nothing there.

"Oh, please, love," Neelix begged, "come out of it! I'm here with you! I'm here . . ."

But she didn't react to him, except to grow suddenly calm. Her eyes drifted shut, and she lay sweating on the bed.

"I've given her a sedative, Neelix," the Doctor said. "She won't waken until I counteract it. I don't want her to injure herself in any way."

"Will that do anything? Will that stop this from happening? It was just terrible! She grabbed me and screamed that she was falling and she'd die if I let go of her. She thought she was tumbling over a cliff or into a pit or a well or something. I just didn't know what to do."

The Doctor straightened briefly, and looked through the sickbay to another area, where Tuvok lay unconscious on another bed. "Yes . . ." Then he looked at Kes again.

"What?" Neelix asked. "Is there some connection between Mr. Vulcan and what's happening to Kes? I heard there was something wrong with him. Is there some illness that she's caught? You have to tell me!"

The Doctor seemed troubled. "I . . . cannot tell you."

"Why not?"

"I promised Kes I would keep this confidential."

"Doctor!" Neelix plowed around the bed to face the Doctor. "You can't keep any secrets about her away from me!"

"Kes requested that I not tell anyone about her condition."

"Her *condition?* Has she got a sickness of some kind?"

"Neelix, please. Under no ethical justification can I speak to anyone about her condition. I am completely obliged by my medical ethics programming. Unfortunately, Kes knew all about it and swore me to doctor-patient confidentiality."

"But what if a decision has to be made? What if she needs something and she can't discuss it with you?"

"As a matter of fact, there already is a decision. It involves the sedation and whether or not I should keep her unconscious. Since I know very little about Ocampa physical and mental traits—"

Neelix held out both hands pleadingly. "There must be some kind of . . . keyhole!"

The Doctor glanced at him. "Loophole. And there is none that I can think of. Only the captain can make a life-or-death decision, and this is not yet a life-or-death situation, at least not to the degree that I can break the confidentiality. Otherwise, I could only discuss the matter with Kes's next of kin. Of course, she has no family on board—"

"Yes, she does!" Neelix pounced. "I'm her next of kin!"

"Neelix . . ."

"It's true! I love her, and she loves me! She asked me to be the father of her child someday! Who else knows her better or cares more about her? Who else? Who on this ship or anywhere?"

The Doctor's very human manifestation of a face

twisted over trouble upon trouble as he tried to think about this and find the keyhole. Loophole.

Neelix clenched his fists and held his breath. As he watched the Doctor try to sort this out, he thought he might as well have been discussing this with a real live person. What an amazing computer thing! An echo of a living person so very real that it felt as if it were alive, and everyone around also felt as if it were living.

Finally the Doctor nodded. To Neelix's fabulous relief, he said, "I accept that."

"Wonderful! Now, tell me what's happening to Kes!"

"Yes . . . well, it has its complicated elements, but I'll try to encapsulate. Mr. Tuvok is experiencing some kind of mental aberration in the form of a little girl's being dropped over a cliff by Tuvok when he was a boy."

"How terrible—what an awful thing to live with."

"Yes, but we're not certain it actually ever occurred. He doesn't have a real memory of it, yet this episode keeps replaying in his mind, sending him into massive physiological and mental reactions. When he first came here, Kes found him and was somehow mentally linked to the same image of the tragic event. But, curiously, her role was different. She actually saw herself as the little girl, while Tuvok saw himself as . . . well, as himself, but as a boy."

Pausing, the Doctor narrowed his eyes and grew quizzical. "Curious . . . perhaps Kes was given the role of the little girl because, in Tuvok's mind, the role of the boy was already taken. What an interesting clue . . ."

"Doctor," Neelix prodded, "what does this have to do with Kes? And what was that you said about the sedative maybe being dangerous for her? Is that what you meant?"

"Yes, I meant that." The Doctor snapped out of his hypothesizing and moved again to Kes's side. "She is an Ocampa. I have no medical records other than those of Kes herself with which to judge Ocampa physiology. I have no comparisons to make, therefore my judgments will be crippled. It seems that sometimes—but not every time—Tuvok experiences a surge of mental activity on this deep level, Kes is drawn into the excitement with him. Probably because of her natural telepathic abilities."

"But she can't even control those! It's like a twitch!"

"I know, but that in itself could be why she's vulnerable. Neelix," the Doctor said, turning to him, "a decision has to be made. With what you know of the Ocampa, you may be able to help make it. Do you accept the risk if the decision is wrong?"

A chill washed through Neelix's body and ran down to his toes. "Yes . . . yes, I accept."

"Very well." The Doctor seemed relieved, if that was possible. "Sedation might be harmful in the case of psychic phenomena. I don't know the peculiarities of Ocampa telepathy. Being sedated might allow her mind to rest, or it may free her to concentrate too heavily on the visions in Tuvok's memory. If she's drawn too completely into the memory, she might actually be overwhelmed by whatever happens to that little girl."

"Like falling off a cliff," Neelix said dimly.

"Yes, like that. We know from past study that dreams can kill. A subject may become so deeply involved in a fantasy that physical reactions occur. Heart attacks, strokes, psychogenic or anaphylactic shock . . . a person can die from this. We must definitely guard against it."

Neelix tried to understand, but these things were not his area of expertise. He was very much a person of the moment, satisfied if the next day or so went well and content not to think beyond it. The idea that one's own mind could actually kill was frightening and foreign. Until now he'd been content to ignore Kes's trickling telepathic talents, because he knew that Kes was good and kind to her core and wouldn't kick a mouse intentionally.

But suddenly he was afraid, wishing she were just an ordinary girl with nothing funny going on.

"Can we," he began, searching for a word, "turn it off?"

The Doctor seemed troubled about that, and looked from Kes to the unconscious Tuvok once again.

"I don't know," he said finally. "We certainly have no science that can abort a telepathic connection. I must be brutally honest with you—I have little hope for Tuvok. His brain isn't reacting well to these episodes or even to the mind-meld therapy the captain is involved with. I have no confidence in this kind of thing. Tuvok's mind is going through some kind of degeneration. What concerns me is that he could take Kes with him."

He looked now at Kes, who seemed to sleep somewhat fitfully under the effects of the sedative.

Watching the Doctor, Neelix found the brutal honesty quite understandable, given that the Doctor was basically a computer compilation of many doctors, but still a computer. He experienced a flash of respect for the Alpha Quadrant people who had built such a machine. They hadn't programmed much of a bedside manner into the Doctor, but he clearly didn't agree with what the captain was doing.

How could "just" a computer think that way?

And somehow this incredible holographic program had been infused with enough . . . what was the word? Humanity? Enough humanity that regret appeared on his face as he gazed down at Kes.

Kes was so precious to Neelix, and now Neelix realized she was precious to the Doctor too. He believed the Doctor's expression, because he couldn't believe the program would be so subtle as to put regret on the Doctor's face just for show. Those clever people had managed to create a computer he would swear was alive.

And Neelix had seen the Doctor treat others, even others who died. He hadn't seen the same kind of concern on the Doctor's face for those others. But Kes was the Doctor's assistant, his pupil, his only constant company. Faced with losing Kes, the Doctor was really worried about her.

Now he could see why Kes talked about the Doctor as she did, as if he were a real person. All this time, Neelix had felt bad that Kes spent most of her time down here in the sterility of sickbay, with only a computer for company, while he himself was up in the galley, mingling with the living crew. He had always imagined she was lonely.

Perhaps she wasn't lonely after all. Perhaps she was the cure for loneliness.

"So the question is whether to leave her sedated or not?" he asked, trying to understand.

"Yes," the Doctor said. "Leaving her sedated may ease the physical trauma, or it may enhance it by taking away her conscious ability to fight the visions. She might actually become too saturated if there is no reality to which she can cling."

"That sounds good to me," Neelix said with a snap of his fingers. "Kes should have part in the decision. If it were me, I would want to be awake and able to face my problem head on."

"Do you accept the risk?" The Doctor was looking at him squarely, plainly wanting Neelix to comprehend something that was far beyond his range.

"Yes," Neelix decided. "Yes, I think Kes would want to be able to wake up and think about this. She should be conscious. Yes. Then I can talk to her and help her work it through."

The Doctor shifted his feet as if they were really sore, and as if he were really troubled. Perhaps he was.

"Very well," he said, and picked up another hypo "I'll bring her out of it. But you know what she'll say."

Neelix drew his perpetually drawn brow. "What will she say?"

"She'll swear us to secrecy on behalf of Tuvok's well-being, just as she maneuvered me into not telling anyone. And she'll be quite displeased with me that I told you."

"I'll make her understand, don't you worry, Doctor. I'll take care of Kes, no matter what it takes."

Rura Penthe.

Janeway knew about that place. The rumors were more mild than the facts, evidently. *Voyager* didn't know it had been flung seventy thousand light-years from home, and it still had in its multiplex brain the logs of those old days of Kirk, Spock, and McCoy and the assassination of Chancellor Gorkon during the Klingons' attempt to make peace for their own sakes.

The chancellor's ship had been hit by a torpedo shot that looked as if it came from the *Enterprise,* which knocked out the artificial gravity on the Klingon ship. While crippled, the ship had been visited by two presumed humans in magnetic gravity boots, who stormed the helpless crew and assassinated Gorkon. When Kirk and his surgeon, McCoy, beamed over to help, the chancellor died under McCoy's hands.

The two officers were accused of conspiracy and assassination, bolted through a government version of "trial," and sent to the gulag of Rura Penthe.

Nobody actually survived Rura Penthe. The keepers there controlled their "criminal" population by tossing "incorrigibles" out into the deadly frozen waste of the planetoid's surface to die under the heatless glow of three distant suns. And almost everybody became "incorrigible" eventually.

Leg irons, jackal-type watch dogs, snowblindness, dark mines and quarries, a snowy wasteland dotted with mummified corpses, despair, and ultimately a painful death. Rura Penitence.

But, typical of James Kirk, a man who had plowed the field of deep space before most others, he had anticipated trouble and had himself dotted with a long-distance locator.

Ah, technology.

So his crew could find him—if they dared cross into Klingon space.

Was that the conversation Captain Sulu and Commander Uhura were actually having? Janeway knew the *Excelsior* headed for Klingon space—did they actually go in? Did the *Enterprise* go?

Unfortunately, the logs didn't provide that rather significant detail. Why not?

The door chime sounded, and her drifting mind snapped back to her own critical reality.

"Come in."

Ensign Harry Kim strode in with his typical expressionless expression, as if he were not too pleased about what he had to report.

"Ensign, what have you found?" Janeway prodded, letting him know that she wasn't in a mood to beat around any bushes.

The young man started to shake his head, then managed not to. "I don't see any connection between this nebula and the one the *Excelsior* saw eighty years ago. This one's a class-seventeen . . . theirs was an eleven. Both contain trace amounts of sirillium, but that's about it."

"But they do *look* similar . . ."

"To the naked eye," Kim told her, "but not to the sensors. Technically, they're very different."

Janeway tried not to look disappointed—after all, her visual-stimulus theory was still operative—but Kim seemed to feel bad about his report.

"You know," he began, faltering, "I've been talking to the Doctor . . . and he tells me it's not unusual for a repressed memory to resurface because of a smell or a visual detail. Maybe the visual similarities between the two nebulas simply triggered Tuvok's memory of the *Excelsior.*"

"But what about the memory of the little girl?" she said instead. "What does she have to do with Tuvok's experiences on board Sulu's ship? The *Excelsior* seems too far removed from that childhood incident . . ."

"Who knows what goes on in a Vulcan's mind?" Kim offered. "Maybe there *is* a connection, and going back to the memory of the *Excelsior* was just an accident, a stray thought Tuvok was having because of the similarities of the two nebulas . . ."

He let his voice trail off, probably because that particular line of logic didn't make any sense and he knew it. Janeway realized he was trying his hardest to help, but there *was* no way to help. Answers couldn't be deduced from facts that wouldn't present themselves.

"You may be right," she said, tossing him a bone. "Nevertheless, I've been studying the *Excelsior* logs—"

"What do they say?"

"Unfortunately, they don't say anything at all."

He blinked. "Nothing?"

She stood up and stretched her legs with a pointless pace around the room.

"It would seem," she said, "that Captain Sulu decided not to enter that journey into his official log. It's full of carefully worded entries and evasive remarks. The day's entry makes some cryptic remark about his ship's being damaged in a gaseous anomaly and needing repairs. Nothing else. He just didn't want anyone to know about what he was doing."

Kim stared at her in his innocent way. "You mean, he falsified his logs?"

Janeway found herself much more forgiving toward Sulu than she ever expected anyone to be toward her.

"It was a very different time, Mr. Kim. Captain Sulu . . . Captain Kirk . . . Dr. McCoy—they all belonged to a different breed of Starfleet officer. I've been reading through their files, and some of the things I found were almost unbelievable."

"They tell stories about Kirk and the *Enterprise* at the Academy," Kim said. "I always thought they were just a bunch of tall tales."

Janeway tilted him a glance. "Haven't you ever heard that truth is stranger than fiction? James Kirk was once held captive by an alien race, and he called the *Enterprise* and ordered them to destroy the entire planet unless he was released within twelve hours."

"You're kidding!"

"And he succeeded. Not only was he released, but he stopped a three-hundred-year-old war that was killing millions. He made a judgment and he stuck with it. Do you know his first officer, doctor, and engineer stuck with him all the way to the end of their careers? And his junior officers were always floating in his periphery. Even when Captain Sulu got his own command, he was always there to back Kirk up."

Kim shook his head. "I can't believe Starfleet let him get away with that."

"It's hard to argue with success, or punish a hero."

"Times sure have changed."

Janeway leaned back against her desk and gazed out at the blue nebula that was giving her such headaches, entertaining unbidden thoughts about the Wild West and the Final Frontier.

"Have you ever read the journals of Captain Christopher Pike or the logs of the *U.S.S. Horizon* and the Federation's first experiences in deep space? They're eye-opening. And they do make you think the past was more exciting than the present. Imagine the era they lived in—the Alpha Quadrant still largely unexplored, humanity on the verge of war with the Klingons, Romulans hiding behind every nebula . . . even the technology we take for granted was still in its early stages. No plasma weapons, no multiphasic shields, their ships were half as fast . . ."

"No replicators," Kim said, "no holodecks . . . you know, ever since I took Starfleet History at the Academy, I always wondered what it would be like to live in those days."

Maybe he was being truthful, or maybe he was throwing the bone back at her, trying to make her feel less alone in this particular series of troubles, but Janeway didn't quite buy the idea that Harry Kim ever really wanted to live in a rougher, tougher time. Chakotay maybe, Tom Paris maybe, but not Kim.

She gazed out the viewport at the open spacescape.

"Space must've seemed a whole lot bigger back then," she quietly mused. "It's not surprising they had to bend the rules a little. They were a little slower to invoke the Prime Directive and a little quicker to pull their phasers."

She found herself smiling into the bejeweled view of space. She understood both those brands of action, being out here so far, virtually alone but for hostile or perplexing presences, going as boldly as she must into places no Federation deciding factor had gone before.

"Of course," she added, clinging to her role in front of Kim, "the whole bunch of them would be booted out of Starfleet today. But I have to admit, I would've loved to ride shotgun at least once with a group of officers like that. The mission is still the same—seek out new life, new civilizations. We're doing a little more of that than we bargained for. We're the legacy of Kirk and Sulu. Sometimes I look out these viewports and realize we're the first human beings to see these stars. It makes me feel . . ."

She gazed out the portal at the swirling nebula, the mindless stars, the beckoning and endless distance. For an instant she was alone in space.

"Sickbay to Captain Janeway."

For a moment she almost didn't answer, didn't want to be disturbed.

"Go ahead, Doctor."

"I'm ready to revive Mr. Tuvok."

"Acknowledged," she said. "I'm on my way."

"Send to Commander, *Enterprise.* 'We stand ready to assist you. Captain Sulu, *U.S.S. Excelsior.*'"

Captain Sulu
Star Trek VI: The Undiscovered Country

CHAPTER

11

"YOUR MIND TO MY MIND . . . YOUR THOUGHTS TO MY thoughts. I am taking us back to the boy I once was . . . the boy lying on the precipice . . ."

Scents of burning insulation. Deck carpet sizzling with ash and sparks. The hot stink of seared conduits still struggling to push electrons through their connections.

That new scent that wouldn't go away for months.

The faint click of a neurocortical monitor. Yes, she could hear that too.

But the smells were her first clues that they weren't on a plateau on Vulcan. She opened her eyes—when had she closed them?—and found herself standing at the science station where Tuvok was assigned. She was back on the bridge of the *Excelsior*.

Red alert lights flashed, and the klaxon whooped.

Smoke stung her eyes and cramped her lungs. The ship bolted and dropped, surged and bucked. Battle!

"Try rerouting power to the containment field!"

"Stabilizing. But I don't know how much longer I can hold her together."

"Targeting array is on manual!"

"Target the lead battle cruiser, full photon spread."

"Firing . . . direct hit to their drive systems. They're dropping out of warp."

"Starboard shields are off-line!"

"Bring us about."

"All stop. Shut down our primary systems." Captain Sulu came forward out of the stenchy smoke.

This was the near end of the battle with the Klingons, exactly the same as the first time she had entered Tuvok's mind. He had come back to the same place again. The same dialogue replayed around Janeway as she looked for Tuvok.

She knew where to look.

There he was, on the command deck, holding the scorched body of Dimitri Valtane.

He laid Valtane on the deck with hopeless finality, then came to join Janeway. His face was creased with the same confusion she felt at having been thrust back here again.

"We're back in the battle with the Klingons," she said. "Eighty years ago."

"I am at a loss to explain, Captain," he attempted. "But it's hard to accept this as a coincidence."

She looked around and stayed quiet, curious about what would happen. This time she wanted to play it out, to see if anything changed that would've affected Tuvok.

"They're closing from all directions, Captain," the helmsman said. "We're surrounded!"

"All stop," Sulu said. "Shut down our primary systems. Warp drive, sensors, tactical, shields—everything except minimal life support."

Rand twisted around. "Sir?"

"We're nearly dead," Sulu told her. "We might as well act like it."

The crew went to work. Gradually the battered supership wheezed to the least of trickling power. Half the lights went off. Systems crackling for attention and beeping for care went suddenly silent.

"All systems are off-line," Rand reported with the calm of defeat. "We're dead in space."

Sulu moved to a console and watched it. "Everyone play possum. Helm . . . as soon as they've closed to within fifty kilometers, I want you to jump to high warp."

Janeway couldn't help a teasing grin. That was the oldest trick in the book. Of course, eighty years ago it wasn't so old yet, was it?

The helmsman looked around at Sulu. "But, sir, with our shields this low, that kind of acceleration might—"

Sulu nodded. "Let's just hope the warp core holds."

A tense pause, and everybody set jaw and waited.

Only Janeway snickered with hindsight. The *Excelsior* class eventually proved itself out as very tough. To these people, the design was fairly new.

They didn't know what a workhorse the class would turn out to be.

The helmsman watched his proximity sensors. "They're closing. Four hundred kilometers . . . three hundred . . . two hundred . . . one hundred . . . fifty kilometers . . ."

Staring, Janeway wondered what the hell Sulu was waiting for—to be able to smell the Klingons' armpits before he took action? Fifty kilometers was spitting distance!

"Engage!" Sulu barked abruptly.

Everybody flinched as if they hadn't been expecting it.

The ship shook, shuddered, and rumbled as the engines shot to high warp like a ball impelled out of a cannon.

Seconds passed.

With a sigh of victory, Rand reported. "We've lost them, sir."

"Back from the dead," Sulu said, congratulating.

Janeway turned to Tuvok. "So that's how he got out of it. He actually used the fact that they had no technology with which to read another ship's warp power-up."

"Yes," Tuvok said tonelessly.

"Tuvok," Janeway said, using his name as a bridge to pull him back to their purpose. "Everything we've seen so far leads up to this moment. Whatever the critical detail is, it occurred sometime before this. I'm betting it had something to do with the Azure Nebula. I want you to go back to the moment when you first saw the nebula. What happened?"

He thought briefly, then told her, "Captain Sulu expected it would take approximately five hours to traverse the nebula and enter Klingon space. He decided that my shift needed some rest, so we returned to the crew quarters . . ."

As if dictated by an unseen magician, the walls around them winked out and turned bright.

Crew quarters. What a surprise.

A few young officers were taking to their bunks. At Janeway's left, Tuvok was on the lower bunk now, with Valtane lounging above on the upper bunk.

She held still a moment. Tuvok's mind was trying to show her something. The least she could do was be polite and watch.

"I attempted to get some sleep," Tuvok said, as if speaking to no one in particular. "But my bunk mate, Dimitri Valtane, felt the need to discuss our situation."

Valtane leaned over the edge of the bunk. "Tuvok? Are you asleep?"

"No."

"Me neither. I can't believe we're really doing this! I didn't think the captain had it in him."

"Had what in him?"

"You know—the guts. To defy orders and go off on a rescue mission to save his old friends."

"I take it from the tone of your voice that you admire this trait," Tuvok said icily.

"Yeah! It's courageous!"

"It is illogical and reckless," the Vulcan insisted. "Which I attempted to point out to him on the bridge."

Valtane looked down again. "Come on, Tuvok. Isn't this more fun than charting gaseous anomalies?"

Tuvok's brows came down on the idea. "The human fascination with 'fun' has led to many tragedies in your short but violent history. One wonders how your race has survived having so much 'fun.'"

Janeway almost spoke up, instead puckering her lips against pointing out that the short but violent history of humanity was also a short but astonishingly productive one that settled and bonded the Alpha Quadrant in just decades, whereas other spacefaring cultures had failed to do that in hundreds of years.

That wouldn't exactly advance the moment, and she needed to follow Tuvok's train of thought, not her own.

Still, she wished she'd really been there.

"Vulcans!" Valtane teased. "You guys need to relax!"

"No," Tuvok decided. "I will not 'relax.' Ever since I entered the Academy, I have had to endure the egocentric nature of humanity. You believe that everyone in the galaxy should be like you. That we should all share your sense of humor and your human values."

Valtane's smile dropped away. "Well, if you hate it here so much, why'd you join Starfleet in the first place?"

Evidently a touchy question, given the changes on Tuvok's face. Was he now the Tuvok of eighty years ago, or was he Janeway's Tuvok playing a role? How much was the role consuming him?

"I joined," he explained, "under pressure from my parents. However, I have already decided to resign my commission once this assignment is complete."

Seeming to have gotten the answer he expected, Valtane leaned back casually and said, "Your loss."

He rolled over and put an end to the conversation that way.

Slowly, Janeway moved to Tuvok's bedside and knelt down, keeping her voice low. Silly—because Valtane couldn't hear her—but she felt there was wisdom in not disturbing Tuvok too much, not creating too much of a chasm between the present and the past when she needed him to keep one foot in each.

"Tuvok," she began, "did you really mean that?"

His brow puckered, as if his second thoughts were encroaching—thoughts from many years yet to come. "At this point in my life . . . yes. My experiences at the Academy and on the *Excelsior* were not pleasant."

"I knew you left Starfleet for more than fifty years, but I never knew why. I didn't realize it was because of a conflict with humans."

"My perception of humanity and Starfleet," he said carefully, "was undoubtedly colored by the fact that I did not want to be here in the first place."

"Your parents really forced you to go to the Academy?"

Parents—she heard her own word echo. Parents had children. Children . . .

"It was their wish," Tuvok went on, not picking up on the fact that she was only half listening now. "And I felt an obligation to fulfill it."

"What did you do during those fifty years?"

"I returned to Vulcan, where I spent several years in seclusion, immersing myself in the Kohlinar, a rigorous discipline intended to purge all emotion. I wanted to attain a state of pure logic."

"What happened?"

"Unfortunately, six years into my studies, I began the *pon farr*. I took a mate."

"T'Pel?"

"Yes. We decided to raise a family together. I chose to postpone my studies."

Feeling a smile tug at her lips, Janeway found it strangely compelling and warm that Tuvok, who had tried to purge away all emotions, chose instead to raise children. The two weren't exactly on the same track.

"And what brought you back to Starfleet?" she asked.

Tuvok paused, considering. Evidently this wasn't something he had thought about for a long, long time. He actually seemed to relax a little.

"Raising children of my own made me appreciate what my parents experienced raising me. And I came to realize that the decisions I made as a youth were not always in my own best interests. I understood their decision to send me to the Academy . . .

and that there were many things I could learn from humans and other species. I decided that I wanted to expand my knowledge of the galaxy. Starfleet," he finished, "provided that opportunity."

She gazed at him. "I'm glad you had a change of heart."

He glanced at her. "As am I, Captain . . . although 'heart' had very little to do with it. It was a logical decision."

"I'm sure it—"

The ship trembled, sending a shiver through Janeway's bones.

Over the comm, Captain Sulu's rumbling voice announced, *"Red alert! All hands to battle stations!"*

The young officers all rolled off their bunks. Valtane came down in a groggy heap, gasping. "What's going on? I thought we were still five hours from Klingon space!"

He took off for the door after the others.

Tuvok stood up. "A Klingon cruiser has decloaked inside the nebula," he said to Janeway. "At this moment, they are firing concussive charges across our bow."

"Let's go," Janeway said, just as another hard shake of the hull nearly slapped her to the deck. If she hadn't had a grip on the edge of the bunk, she'd have gone down. Fine thing, sprain an ankle in the middle of an illusion.

So which doctor would do a better job treating it? The illusionary doctor of a distant memory, or the holographic doctor of twenty-fourth-century technology?

Hmmm . . .

The smells of the bridge encroached on Janeway as she and Tuvok blended again onto the *Excelsior's* bridge. Was his mind rushing them around, or were her own thoughts beginning to fuse?

She'd seen this before—the bridge before the battle with the Klingons. Sulu at the command center, Valtane at his post, Rand at hers, Tuvok at his—

There, however, was something she hadn't seen before. A Klingon filling the main screen.

"Mr. Sulu," the Klingon was saying. "I see they've finally given you the captaincy you deserve. Don't let it end prematurely."

Calm and affable, but unflapped, Sulu didn't flinch from the Klingon's glare. "Kang," he greeted as if they were passing in a hallway. "We've been on a survey mission studying this nebula. Our navigation systems malfunctioned. And I'm afraid we got lost."

Janeway took the moment to move about the bridge and look at the readouts. The battle would begin soon. What kind of precautions did a ship like this take?

"Well, you've been found," the Klingon said intolerantly. "I suggest you abandon your 'survey' mission, reverse course, and leave this area immediately."

"As soon as we've completed repairs," Sulu said fluidly, "we'll be on our way."

"We'd be happy to escort you back to Federation space."

It was not an offer, but an order.

"Very generous of you," Sulu said. "But we can manage."

"I insist."

Janeway knew that tone. This Klingon wasn't backing down. She paused and watched Sulu.

"Actually," the twenty-third-century captain said, "an escort would be welcome. We'd hate to lose our way again."

Not bad, Janeway thought. Let them think they have the upper hand. Give them what they want.

She tried to measure up the armaments of the Klingon ship being dissected by sensors all over the screens around her, but she had little basis for comparison. She wasn't familiar with Klingon vessels' firepower from eighty years ago.

Kang was smiling, assuming he'd won. "Bring your ship about, bearing one-eight-one mark two."

"Nice to see you again, Kang," Sulu said, just before the communication was cut off at the source.

The main screen flashed to a view of the cloying Azure Nebula all around them, pinwheeling around the presence of Kang's Klingon battle cruiser.

Valtane turned. "Captain?"

"Man your station, Lieutenant," Sulu said passively. "We're not giving up just yet. Helm, come about."

The view changed as the ship slowly swung full about, and the main screen shifted to a departure angle, showing the Klingon ship following them at slightly less than respectful distance.

"Tactical status?" Sulu requested.

Valtane checked his sensors. "They have their forward disruptors trained on us, sir."

Janeway huffed. Sure, they needed sensors to tell them that.

Sulu started pacing the bridge, stalking a way out of this situation, making quite obvious the fact that he didn't intend to stay in this predicament. Janeway found herself thinking up ways out too, and wondered which one he would try.

"Ensign Tuvok," Sulu began, "what's the composition of this nebula?"

Tuvok checked his own controls. "Primarily oxygen and argon, plus traces of theta-xenon, sirillium gas, and fluorine."

"Sirillium . . . that's a highly combustible substance, isn't it?"

Ah—Janeway smiled. Her third choice was his first.

"Affirmative," Tuvok said stiffly as he got the idea of what his captain—his first captain—had in mind.

"Is there any way we could ignite the sirillium?" Sulu asked, even though he didn't really need to explain it to anybody there. Perhaps he just wanted to confirm in all their minds what his intention was.

Tuvok drew a breath. "If we modulated a positron beam to a subspace frequency," he said, letting the breath out slowly, "it would trigger a thermochemical reaction in the sirillium."

Sulu smiled. "Like tossing a match into a pool of gasoline. Would their shields withstand the blast?"

"Yes, but their sensors and tactical systems would be disrupted for several seconds."

"That's all the time we need."

Interesting, Janeway thought, that Sulu had considered the survival of his enemies, who obviously wouldn't return the favor. Or perhaps he was being even more practical—avoiding destroying Klingon nationals just to untwist a twisted moment. Janeway lauded his prudence as much as his boldness.

Bold, yes, because the violent escape would virtually prove that he wasn't here because of any nav malfunction.

Of course, Kang already knew that.

"Tuvok," Sulu went on, "modulate a positron beam and stand by. We'll ignite the sirillium the instant we clear the nebula. Helm, prepare to engage maximum warp on my command."

"Aye, sir," the Halkan at the helm said.

Valtane, Tuvok, and the others plunged to work, and Sulu took his command chair.

"All hands," he said, "this is the captain. Secure stations and batten down the hatches."

Tuvok straightened from his controls. "The positron beam is charged and ready."

"Oh my mark, Ensign."

Janeway wondered how far out of the nebula Sulu would try to go before igniting the sirillium. All attention fell to Valtane, who was watching the proximity monitors.

"We're clearing the nebula," Valtane said evenly, and from his measured tone Janeway could tell they were *barely* clearing the nebula.

"Mr. Tuvok," Sulu said, definitely enjoying himself, "light the match."

An energy beam vaulted from the big ship's stern into the gushing blue nebula, a few degrees sideways from where the Klingon ship was just becoming visible. The gaseous cloud gulped the energy, began glowing a weird yellow-green right where the beam penetrated, then lit up with a fabulous explosive flash made mostly of glowing white and blue particles.

The Klingon ship was jarred severely and fell off its course, wobbling on a wing and sinking some against its own axis.

"The Klingon ship's been disabled," Valtane reported with victory in his voice. "They're not pursuing!"

"Helm," Sulu said, not bothering with self-congratulation, "set a course for Kronos and engage."

The ship came about in a sweeping arch and skimmed the Azure Nebula back to face Klingon space again.

"Commander Rand," Sulu began, "I want you to—"

An alarm interrupted him from Valtane's console.

"Sir!" Valtane called. "Long-range sensors are detecting three Klingon battle cruisers on an intercept course! They're arming torpedoes!"

CHAPTER

12

"CHAKOTAY TO SICKBAY."

"Sickbay."

"Doctor, in your opinion, what's the progress of that melding experiment?"

"My opinion? I have nothing with which to compare something like this, Commander. Mr. Tuvok's mental state is tenuous, his brain stability losing integrity, and there's a steady downward digression."

"I see. Tell me this—you don't think there's any attachment physically to that nebula out there?"

"At the moment, I have nothing to suggest that, other than a possible visual trigger involving Mr. Tuvok."

"So I'm probably safe in going ahead with the sirillium collection?"

"Your call, Commander."

"All right, thank you. Bridge out."

At the helm, Tom Paris was looking at him. "Well?"

Chakotay gave him a scolding, narrow-eyed glare and refused to say anything.

"Well, *sir,*" Paris accommodated. "Are we going after the sirillium or not?"

From the bridge engineering station, B'Elanna Torres stepped to the edge of the upper platform. "If it doesn't affect Mr. Tuvok or the captain, there's no reason to wait. We can start scooping sirillium any minute."

Chakotay gazed at the main view, still showing the turbulent blue nebula roiling before them. "What if this belongs to somebody else?"

"Belongs?" Paris repeated with a crimp of his features. "It's just sitting there!"

"Yes, but one thing I've discovered is that in a populated area of space, there's no untapped resource. Chances are pretty dim that nobody's noticed the sirillium source."

"All the more reason," B'Elanna said, "to get cracking, get the sirillium, and get out of here."

"I tend to agree. After all, I don't see any 'No Trespassing' buoys."

Torres stepped down to his level. "But I do have one suggestion."

"And that is?"

"There's a particularly rich vein in there, about six hundred kilometers in and slightly to the starboard of where we are now. If we could go into that area, we could scoop out more sirillium in a couple of hours than we could mining the whole nebula for a month."

"But . . ."

She seemed annoyed that he was reading her so well. "But," she allowed, "it's also turbulent enough to turn the ship on its ear. We'd have our hull plates rattled off within ten minutes."

"So much for two hours. You have an alternative, I'll bet."

"Yes, I do. A shuttlecraft."

"You want me to send a shuttlecraft into turbulence so violent that a starship can't navigate it?" He said it, but sometimes stating the incredibly obvious was a command prerogative. He knew she had this all thought out, but making senior officers sweat was another one.

Torres kept the annoyance out of her voice on purpose, because she knew he was tightroping her on purpose. "A shuttlecraft has only a small fraction of the hull and mass of a starship. There's just less to kick around, and movements are quicker, compensations easier, and we can just go in and ride the waves without trying to fight them. We can pull a position scoop behind us, power into the nebula to the dense vein, then power down and just roll around, collecting sirillium. When we've got all we can carry, the ship can enable tractor beams and pull us out."

"Are you volunteering, B'Elanna?"

She crossed her arms, and her Klingon defiance bubbled to the top. "What else does 'us' mean?"

"Who's the other half of 'us'?"

She shrugged one shoulder. "Doesn't matter, except I need a quick-fingered pilot."

At the helm, Chakotay could see Paris grin. "Mr. Paris?"

Paris shook his head, then swiveled around and stood up. "Sir," he said, "this is me volunteering."

Chakotay felt a smile tug, but resisted it. "Very well. We'll hold position here. You prepare the shuttlecraft and—"

"It's already mounted with the scoop and storage tanks," Torres told him. "I presumed you'd agree, so I had the work done an hour ago. All we have to do is launch."

Paris sighed. "No time to write a will, I guess, then?"

"Dismissed," Chakotay said.

As Torres went without a backward glance to the turbolift, Paris followed, muttering, "Doesn't matter . . . what've I got to leave to anybody? And who've I got to leave it to? Just a simple adventurer bequeathing to future generations a legacy of greatness and wonder . . ."

"Tom Paris," Chakotay finished. "Legend in his own mind."

As the turbolift opened, Harry Kim stepped out just in time to have his hand seized and shaken by Paris.

"Harry, old pal," Paris said. "Take care of the ship after I'm gone. I know you can do it. Remember me fondly, and give Lieutenant Nicoletti my fond regards, will you? Tell her it just wasn't meant to be."

"What?" Kim stared at the closing lift doors. "Tom?"

But the doors closed, clipping off one last look of sorrowful nobility from Paris and a roll of the eyes from Torres.

Baffled, Kim turned to Chakotay. "Sir? Why's Tom leaving the bridge? It's not change of watch yet."

"No," Chakotay said. "They're going out on a shuttlecraft into the nebula."

Kim's fresh-faced expression buckled. "Into *that?* We can't even get the *Voyager* through that!"

"Exactly why we're sending the shuttle. There's less bulk to knock around. I want you to monitor the shuttlecraft's every movement and have the tractor beam ready to pull them out. Also, adjust your sensor monitors to give us a reading of the amount and density of sirillium being transferred into the tanks. Be ready to move on a moment's notice. No matter how fast we work, it'll take several minutes to yank them back. I don't want any delays. Those two shouldn't stay out there any longer than absolutely necessary."

"Yes, sir . . . right away." Kim frowned and headed to his post as if wondering whether or not they really needed sirillium all this badly.

Chakotay felt sorry for the young officer as he watched Kim work his consoles. This was the risk of joining an outfit like Starfleet. Make a friend, send him out into risk, possibly lose him. Hesitate about making friends the next time.

Lose a friend, lose a captain—maybe both. Perhaps this was why many Starfleet crews over the years had learned to keep an arm's length between each other. The captain and Tuvok were supposedly friends, and look what it was getting them. The captain might be dragged down into that swirling mental muck with Tuvok, too deeply ever to pull out again.

Chakotay sighed. Sometimes he wanted to go sit on a rock and just sit.

"Torres to bridge."

"Chakotay."

"We're about to launch. I'm going to start feeding readings through to you right now."

"Acknowledged. Feed them through to Mr. Kim's tactical monitors. Mr. Kim?"

"Ready, sir."

"Go ahead, B'Elanna."

"Acknowledged. Beginning feed . . . and launching."

Holding his breath without even realizing he was doing it, Chakotay clenched his jaw and watched as the shuttlecraft looped up from under *Voyager*'s port belly and plunged headlong into the depths of the blue nebula. At first, the shuttlecraft seemed to be steady on its course. Then it surged into a choppy swirl and started twisting against its own course.

"Shuttle's power grid is flickering," Kim reported. "It doesn't like whatever's out there."

Chakotay glanced at him. "Give them a few minutes. They've got their hands full."

He watched until he couldn't see the small dot anymore, and was glad the sensors could still see it.

Looked awfully small out there in that chewing mass of energy. What if there were gravity wells hiding in that mess? The shuttle's thin hull would be crushed like a rotten melon.

Too late. Should've thought of that ten minutes ago.

Damn.

"Mr. Kim?" he prodded when he couldn't stand the silence anymore.

"They're still alive, sir."

Not exactly the response he was hoping for. Something a little more technical would've been reassuring this time. Chakotay watched the screen, as if he could hold on to the shuttlecraft if he could only see it.

"Shuttlecraft to Voyager." Paris's voice came over the comm with a notable rasp as the signal bucked interference from inside the tumbling, unfriendly nebula.

"Chakotay here. What are the conditions, Mr. Paris?"

"Some very rough seas in here. B'Elanna's running around in the shuttle like a—"

"Don't you dare continue that."

"Well, she's running around. The scoop is deploying and I'm about to shut down engine thrust, so we'll be tumbling around with the strongest waves. Theoretically, that'll automatically take us through the most dense sirillium deposits. Be aware that once I shut down the engines I won't be able to restart them again in the middle of this soup, not without igniting

the sirillium. If you can't pull us out with your tractor beams, we'll just be a kind of weird Christmas ornament rolling around inside this thing just about forever."

Chakotay felt his stomach tighten. "Acknowledged. We'll get you out if we have to come in and throw a net over you."

"And who's going to throw a net over you, then?"

"You let me worry about that."

"Oh, no, Commander, I can share. After I shut down, there won't be anything for me to do out here but worry."

"I'm sure B'Elanna will keep you busy. What's your planned course?"

"I'm powering straight into the vein to the far side, then I'm going to loop around so our thrust is pushing us back toward you. That's when I'll cut engines. With a little luck, the corkscrew currents we're reading in there will keep moving us along the same general direction until you can pick us up visually. At that point we'll let you know if we can stand to stay out here any longer, or if our tanks are full. If you can see us but not contact us, I'd suggest you bring us back without confirmation."

"Understood. Tractor beam is standing by."

"B'Elanna says she's ready to start collecting the sirillium. Coming about to course one-four-four in three . . . two . . . one . . . mark. Engine shutdown in five seconds. Five . . . four . . ."

"Sir," Harry Kim spoke up, "I can read the corkscrew wave he's entering, and I think I have a fix on the shuttlecraft, but there are a lot of sensor echoes out there. I'm losing him every few seconds and having to reacquire."

"Do your best, Mr. Kim. Stay on top of it. We might have to change plans any second."

"Trying, sir."

"Engines off—whoa!"

Chakotay leaned forward. "Paris, report!"

The comm fritzed and squawked for about five seconds, then, *"Really rough out here . . . really rough. Makes me wish I was back in that penal colony, serving a nice, safe sentence. Next time Captain Janeway offers me a chance for a new start, remind me to twist her bun a little tighter."*

"That's disrespectful, mister," Chakotay reminded. "Stick to your job."

"Yes, sir. Right now I'm stuck to the shuttle's port—bulkhead. B'Elanna says the sirillium collection's going as planned—so far. Stress on the hull is—increasing. Hope we hold together. Sir, I have to leave the helm to help stabilize the tanks."

"Keep the shuttle's comm lines open, Paris. Your commbadges won't carry through that interference."

"Standing by."

Chakotay glanced at the sensor monitor on the starboard side, the one showing a schematic of the turbulence patterns. There was little sense to be made by the constant churning, and if Paris and Kim could detect a corkscrew pattern, more power to them. So far the ship itself was holding steady.

He hoped everything continued to go this well.

And without meaning to, he started to think of sickbay, of Tuvok, and of the captain.

"Are they still in that . . . that . . . weld?"

"Meld," Kes said with a tolerant smile. Neelix was so gentle, and so very unscientific.

Together they gazed through the clear partition from the lab to the main ward, where the captain and Tuvok were once again sitting face-to-face, with Tuvok's hands on the captain's face. Pressure points, Mr. Tuvok had explained to Kes. Changes of nerve connections. Other things. The Vulcan meld was partly physical, as well she had found out.

Neelix was watching her—she could feel his eyes as she worked.

After a moment she had to look up. "Neelix," she began with a little push of encouragement, "I'm fine. You don't have to keep watching me. Before long you're going to have to go start lunch for the next watch, aren't you?"

"Yes," he said unhappily. "But I'd rather not go. I don't like leaving you here with . . . well, that. Him. Them. Like that."

"Tuvok?"

"Yes, Tuvok! Kes—please. Let me take you away. They'll lend us a shuttle. Let's go away from the ship until all this is over. Please."

"Neelix, we don't know how far away this can still affect me. It's a telepathic bond, not a physical one. There's no way to know whether distance will have any effect."

"But the connection's growing and becoming harder on you. You look so tired already. Maybe the others can't tell, but I can. When I hold you, I can tell your heart's pounding. You're shivering. You're very brave, my love, but this is putting terrible stress on you that maybe a Vulcan can take, but you're not Vulcan. You're not."

"The Doctor's been giving me suppressants to control my reactions." She tried to go back to her work, but his sweet concern was distracting. "I can't even leave the sickbay. I'm under restriction."

"We'll get permission!"

"They need me, Neelix."

"Kes . . ." He caught her arm and drew her away from the console. "This isn't right. I demand that this mind thing be broken."

"We don't even know whether that can help me," she told him, letting herself become forceful to match his concerned irrationality. "We don't know anything about this. Tuvok's mind is degrading—" Then she realized she'd said the wrong thing and quickly said, "Other than the captain's succeeding, the only thing we know will break this is Tuvok's death. Doesn't that mean anything to you?"

"Right now, it means *you* to me," he said, clasping her by both arms. Beyond the love in his eyes, a terrible, desperate anger rose. "Kes, Tuvok has lived more than a hundred years! You've only lived two!"

Goodness, his face was a clatter of emotions. How sweet and charming to be the one for whom he had all these feelings.

But the meaning of his words and the anger behind his eyes made her unable to receive the love at this particular moment. She returned his grip with a grip of her own upon his shoulders.

"Are you willing to do it?" she demanded.

He stared at her. "Do what?"

She reached to one side and picked up a hypo. What was inside didn't matter for the point she was trying to make. "Will you do it? Go to Tuvok and kill him?"

Neelix stood back from the hypo, his hands at his sides, and stared at it.

Kes shook it before him. "That's what you're talking about, isn't it? This will do it, Neelix."

She summoned the tough shield she had seen others on this ship use to protect themselves from their own fears when danger demanded their resolve. There wasn't much she could do for these people, these strangers from another part of the galaxy who had risked their lives for her, saved her, embraced her, and given her purpose.

"This is the only way," she told him gently, but firmly. "We're part of this crew now. We have to stand together. Tuvok can't take the stress all by himself. I've got to do this for him. Maybe I'm helping purge some of this in some way. I have to take it, for his sake, just as he would for mine." She stepped toward him, lowering the hypo. "And I can't take the stress of worrying about what you're going to do, Neelix. I have to know you'll hold to your promise and say nothing about this to anyone. It's my decision. Promise me. Promise me, Neelix. Or things will be forever changed between us."

CHAPTER

13

"MAINTAIN COURSE."

Captain Hikaru Sulu didn't seem surprised that Klingons had appeared, but did seem oddly irritated that his plans were compromised by the hostile race's defense of their own territory. Apparently he'd made his decision and was staying the course.

Did he really intend to go all the way to the Klingon homeworld, or perhaps to Rura Penthe itself, and effect the rescue personally? Or was he making a show, distracting Klingon firepower and attention away from whatever the *Enterprise* was doing on its own?

Janeway had her own suspicions. Was Sulu actually expecting to beat back three Klingon cruisers?

No—that didn't make sense. If he'd wanted his

presence in the vicinity to remain secret, he would've destroyed Kang's ship straight off. But he hadn't—in fact, he'd given them plenty of time to send off their communication to these three. Now four of the Klingon's main fleet vessels were involved with the *Excelsior,* instead of somewhere else. If Janeway remembered correctly, the whole Klingon fleet was comprised of only about ten heavy cruisers.

And four were here.

Sulu was creating a diversion. That had to be the answer.

The ship went into warp maneuvering at almost the same instant as the Klingon ships started firing volleys of torpedoes. The *Excelsior* rocked viciously, but held her course straight back toward the depths of Klingon space, ensuring that these Klingons would be nice and mad, and concentrating right here, right now.

"Return fire!" Sulu finally freed his crew to react, now that he had allowed the Klingons to get nice and close, close enough to be fully engaged and not veer off casually. He wanted their full attention and was willing to risk his ship to get it.

In person, as if invited by command request, Captain Kathryn Janeway witnessed just the kind of bootstrap resolve she'd only imagined in these captains of the last century. She found herself enjoying it, even learning. She thought those days of command surprises were over for her.

But, of course, she'd yet to participate in a full-blown war on a long-term basis, or the touchy beginnings of a war, or even the touchy beginnings of peace. She found herself hungry to keep watching.

"Evasive pattern Delta-Six," Sulu dictated, suddenly very calm.

"Aye, Captain," the helmsman said. "Evasive pattern Delta-Six."

At tactical, Rand said, "They're closing to two thousand kilometers. Three more vessels are coming within sensor range!"

Valtane sucked a hard breath. "Captain, torpedoes incoming, aft and forward!"

"Shipwide alert—all hands, brace for impact."

The ship bolted hard to port and down a full ten degrees, dropping the deck out from under her and the struggling crew. Janeway wished she could do something, but—

Six—seven Klingon vessels!

"Direct hit," Rand gasped. "Port bow. Shields down to twenty percent. Losing atmosphere on decks five, six, and seven."

Suddenly a blur of voices overwrote her voice.

"Try rerouting power to the containment field!"

"Stabilizing, but I don't know how much longer I can keep her together—"

"Target the lead battle cruiser, full photon spread."

"Firing weapons . . . direct hit to their drive system. Lead battle cruiser is dropping out of warp."

"Bring us about."

"Full about, aye."

"Captain!" Valtane called. "They've knocked out our targeting scanners—"

"Switch to manual," Sulu returned as if teaching a class.

Valtane ran from his control console to a console near Tuvok and started picking at it, trying to be careful despite the kicking and shaking.

"Rupture in plasma conduit One-Bravo. It will not hold much longer." Tuvok wrestled with his own console, fully involved in the moment as it unrolled before him, with every bit the conviction Janeway had come to expect of him on her own ship. Would that alter this memory? Tuvok, the experienced security officer a hundred years old handling a starship's console, rather than Tuvok the twenty-nine-year-old ensign with only two months' experience? Would that make any difference?

This was such an inexact science—and she'd heard some of this dialogue before, but not in this order. How did things really happen eighty years ago? Was Tuvok remembering correctly? Or were these memories becoming jumbled?

Tuvok looked at his console, looked at Valtane's, worked his own with both hands, then looked at Valtane's board again.

"Mr. Valtane, there's a rupture in the plasma conduit behind your console—get away from that station."

Valtane started sweating so hard that his black hair matted. "One more second . . ."

Tuvok worked more on his own board, but kept

one eye on Valtane's, and he was right from what Janeway could see from where she was standing, clinging to a chair.

Suddenly Valtane's board began crackling under its molded surface.

Tuvok shouted, "Dimitri, you must—"

Too late. The console exploded in a shower of sparks.

"Almost complete," Harry Kim said. "Sirillium containment tanks are about full. We should be able to get a visual of the shuttle any second now, sir." The ensign looked up at the main viewscreen in anticipation. "I hope they're stable. With tanks full of sirillium, that shuttle's a floating bomb."

The turbolift door sounded, and Kes charged onto the bridge while Chakotay was standing over Kim's tactical board, watching the erratic movements of the shuttlecraft as it slammed back and forth like a child's body in a water chute.

He straightened. "Kes? Something wrong?"

She didn't respond, but only stared at the forward screen just as the gray dot of the shuttlecraft made its first appearance.

At first, Chakotay thought something had gone wrong with the captain or Tuvok, or both, but why would Kes come all the way up here to tell them something that could've been told over the comm system?

But she didn't look at him, didn't look at anyone, except at the main screen.

Well, if she just wanted to watch . . .

The shuttlecraft, twisting and tumbling, came toward them, gaining miles by the second, pushed along by the strong surges of energy inside the dense sirillium vein. Behind it, it dragged the parachute-shaped position scoop, five times the diameter of the shuttle itself, carving out huge tracks of sirillium and funneling it through the containment system into the tanks. Even farther behind, the shuttle left a glittering, hostile trail of agitated sirillium tracings and other active substances. Chakotay tightened his eyes in empathy for Paris and B'Elanna, being tossed about like shrapnel in high wind, dragging high explosive. They'd survive, but they'd be plenty bruised.

"There they are!" Kim blurted tightly, tense and relieved at the same time.

Chakotay took a breath to order the tractor beams on, but before anything came between his lips, Kes suddenly charged to the unmanned helm and dropped into the seat. At first, this was an innocent enough move because she didn't know how to drive the ship anyway.

But she scanned the board once quickly, then tapped a critical control.

"Phasers armed!" Kim gasped. "Kes! Don't!"

"Kes!" Chakotay lunged toward her, his hand outstretched to grab her by the shoulder just as she reached for the firing controls.

He didn't make it. She did.

Pfew pfew pfew—the phasers stabbed into the blue

nebula, igniting the sirillium traces still left around the shuttle, until the shuttle was engulfed in crackling mini-explosions.

Only by luck, the phasers weren't targeted and Kes hadn't hit the shuttle itself. Otherwise, one big boom would overwrite the noble end of Paris and Torres.

But the phaser beams chopped through the combustible nebula and scratched the shuttle, which was sucked into the trail of ignition by the collapsing currents. Chemical and turbulence force changes inside the nebula, caused by the eruptions of billions of sirillium molecules, caused negative pressure areas that dragged currents in, and the shuttle with them.

It took Chakotay four steps to make it down to the helm, and that wasn't soon enough to stop the firing pattern from playing out. Three phaser blasts cut out from the forward hull of *Voyager,* creasing the nebula with billions of detonations in long sizzling trails, and kicking the shuttle around like a football.

"Kes!" Chakotay yanked her physically out of the chair and sent her tumbling to the deck rather cruelly. "Why did you do that?"

Her normally placid eyes, so like a painting, were tortured and wide. "They attacked us! We have to return fire! They killed Valtane!"

Harry Kim looked over his console. "Kes, that's Tom and B'Elanna out there!"

"Yes!" Kes threw him a fiery glare. "She's a Klingon! We have to return fire!"

Chakotay snapped his fingers and summoned Lieutenant Carey from the upper deck engineering station. "Carey, take her to sickbay! Make sure the Doctor keeps her there."

"Aye, sir." The engineer took Kes by both arms and steered her without much effort off the bridge.

"Kang did this!" Kes shouted. "He must've notified the Empire! We have to fire again!"

"Out," Chakotay said to Carey, and in a moment the lift doors murmured closed.

"What was that all about?" Kim asked.

"Condition of the shuttlecraft!" Chakotay barked. "Are they alive?"

Kim played his board for a few seconds. "Picking up some debris . . . but only bits. No sufficient mass for a shuttlecraft, but I can't pick up their trail. I've lost contact, sir!"

The stink was ungodly as Lieutenant Valtane was blown backward and slammed into the deck.

Tuvok left his post, an action that spoke for itself.

Sparks continued to rain upon him and the unfortunate Valtane as Tuvok gathered his bunk mate into his arms.

No emotions? Then whence came the notice of final comfort?

Janeway realized that this was a moment she had yet to see. She'd been here before it and after it, but this particular few seconds, critical for Tuvok and for Valtane if not for the ship and its captain, had been evading her.

Now she was here for it, and she was deeply moved. This might be the first time Tuvok had ever witnessed the death of a crewmate, never mind a bunk mate. No one, Vulcan, human, or any other, could go unmoved from that and call himself alive.

Valtane's eyes stared, and his lips moved. Was he trying to speak? Would he speak words critical to Janeway's own problem? She started to step closer, to encroach upon the supremely private moment, when Valtane's eyes glazed and a wince of pain cut off his murmuring.

A hand of dizziness passed before Janeway's eyes, blurring the forms of the two young men on the deck. She wobbled and leaned back on the console, disoriented. Was the meld cracking again?

"Tuvok . . . what . . ."

A dog barked in the near distance.

Dog? On a starship?

It sounded like her childhood pet, Bramble.

Her vision cleared, and she could discern her dog galloping through a familiar corn field, even though she was standing on the Johnsons' hill next to their pole barn. She could usually see almost any movement from up here . . .

What was Tom Paris doing on the Johnsons' farm?

"I have no problem helping you track down my friends in the Maquis, Captain," he said. "All I need to know is, what's in it for me?"

She almost hit him.

In fact, she reached out. If she were only closer, she could help him get the girl back up over the cliff. Maybe she could change what had happened . . . but she wasn't even alive when this occurred. The plateau—Tuvok as a child—almost a hundred years ago . . .

"Tuvok!" The child's pitiful scream pierced Janeway's mind.

His hand was so small, almost as small as the girl's. He couldn't possibly have the strength to pull her up.

But he could let go now—Valtane was dead, and nothing could help. Tuvok looked up and saw Janeway, and stared in abject shock.

Janeway reached out to him, but she may as well have been a hundred feet away. She wanted to help, but her mind wouldn't allow her access to the memory.

Memory? Or had this turned into some kind of weird time travel? Was she really here? Were psychic transferences possible? Could she be proving a thousand-year-old myth here and now?

"Tuvok!"

The little girl shrieked again. And Tuvok lost his grip.

As Tuvok and Janeway watched helplessly, the tiny Vulcan child tumbled into the jaws of the rocks below.

If this was a dream or a vision, it was one hell of a vicious one.

Kes felt weak but aware as the engineer dragged her back to the sickbay and hustled her to where the Doctor was rushing from console to console, trying to settle the captain's and Tuvok's brain activity down.

"Kes," the Doctor said, "what's wrong? Did you have another of those episodes?"

"She came onto the bridge," the engineer said, "and fired the phasers at our own shuttlecraft. Said something about firing at Klingons and B'Elanna was a Klingon."

"B'Elanna Torres *is* half Klingon," the Doctor mentioned pointlessly.

Carey huffed and said, "But she's our own chief engineer! Mr. Chakotay says for you to keep Kes in sickbay. I suggest you use the sickbay's automatic bio-security system."

"Yes," the Doctor agreed, eyeing Kes. "I'll do that."

"I've got to go." Carey headed for the door. "We've got a rescue on our hands, and it's gonna be a bitch."

"I didn't mean to," Kes murmured. "I was trying to help!"

"You helped, okay? We'll handle it."

"But B'Elanna and Tom . . . what've I done!" Fear charged through her for her shipmates—not just fear, but dementia. What must Tuvok be going through? She tried to imagine having done what Tuvok had done, spending nearly a century training his mind, only to have it turn on him.

After Mr. Carey was gone, she turned to the Doctor. "I have to hold on," she said with passion. "I didn't mean to hurt anyone. If I try anything else, you have to stop me."

"I understand," the Doctor told her. "You're not responsible for any of this. I've activated the selective bio-security system. If you attempt to leave sickbay, you'll be mildly stunned. Do you understand?"

"Oh," she said empathically, "believe me, after what just happened, I don't even want to leave."

"Kes," the Doctor added, "medical ethics don't require you to sacrifice yourself for a patient. Perhaps we could—"

"But I've learned," she interrupted, "that sometimes they do demand I risk myself for a crewmate. Now that others have been hurt, we have to try even harder to fix all this. I wish I could help B'Elanna and Tom somehow—"

"You can't. You'd do them a favor to stay here and let Mr. Chakotay and the others do their own jobs to save those two. You and I will concentrate on our own problem. After all, this is the one we perhaps *can* solve."

Steadied somewhat now, Kes nodded and turned her attention to the place where she could do some good. "Why are the alarms going off on the captain and Tuvok?"

She gestured at the two mind-melded people and the chittering alarms flashing on the cortical monitors.

"Something's happening inside the meld," the Doctor told her. "There's terrible degradation occurring."

"Why can't I feel it? Why was I let go from the connection?"

The Doctor shook his head. "There's no way to know that. Tuvok's mind may be shutting down different places in his brain, attempting to regain control. You may have been released, but there's no way to tell when or whether you'll be engulfed again."

Troubled, Kes hurried to Tuvok and the captain, frustrated that she couldn't just reach out and touch them, shake them out of the terrible visions.

Suddenly the alarm changed pitch, and the brain patterns on the screens started fluxing.

"What's happening?" she asked.

She wished she had the authority to turn off the terrible alarms ringing from the two monitors and the erratic brain patterns snowing on the monitors—how disturbing!

Mr. Tuvok and the captain were sitting together, facing each other, staring and frozen as if someone had sprayed them with fixative.

The Doctor rushed to the two subjects, and Kes held her breath.

"Their memory engrams are destabilizing," he said with a touch of mystery. Then he frowned and tried to read the panicked information on the monitors. "Something must be going wrong with the mind-meld."

He scowled again at a thing he didn't really understand, aggravated possibly because he himself was a computer generation and at his core was guided by the sense and numbers of a machine that believed in concrete answers.

There was nothing, nothing, and nothing concrete about the Vulcan mind-meld.

"I'm going to bring them out of it," he decided.

He seemed relieved that medical necessity now removed the choice from himself, or Kes, or even Chakotay.

He tapped some controls on a panel Kes had long ago been told never to touch. She couldn't help a moment of fascination and awe at her new chosen career—medical science—and she realized there was still so much she had yet to learn. In her short life, would she have time to learn it all?

Did anyone? Even creatures whose life spans were longer than nine years?

Even the Doctor here, who was in essence a compilation of all doctors and all knowledge where this ship came from, was learning new things by the day.

Kes watched—the Doctor was frowning again. She came around and looked at the monitors. "It's not working."

"Their neural patterns appear to be locked together. I can't break the meld."

He checked another reading, genuinely frustrated by his inability to stop what was happening.

"The damage to Tuvok's synaptic pathways is accelerating. At this rate, he'll be brain-dead within twenty minutes." He tapped a single activator, then urgently added, "Get me the cortical stimulator!"

CHAPTER

14

"PARIS! TOM! WAKE UP. WE'RE IN TROUBLE."

"My head . . ."

"The containment system is agitated! We've got eruptions of sirillium deposits all around us for more than eighty kilometers! We can't clear it unless you get up and help me!"

"My shoulder . . . am I bleeding?"

"Yes, you're bleeding. You fell into an open conduit cover. You've got a slash across the outside of your shoulder. If we live, we'll stop it. Try to get up."

"Warm and tender as ever, B'Elanna. I can always count on—oh, my ribs!"

"Don't push your luck. *Voyager!* Do you read us? *Voyager,* come in!"

Torres pushed away from Paris, who looked a lot worse than he sounded, and punched the communication's surge controls. They had to communicate if they were going to get out, and they had to have power if they were going to communicate.

Every few seconds a new scatter of explosions outside bumped the shuttle into a new surge pattern, and it shook as if running on a cracked track.

"The sirillium's been ignited." Torres gasped, choking on coolant leakage and compromised atmospheric integrity. *"Voyager,* why did you fire on us?"

She stumbled back to Paris and picked at the containment tank controls over his head as he lay on the deck.

"It must've been a malfunction," she decided. "The phasers ignited the residual sirillium. We're just lucky we'd collected most of it before they fired, or we'd be real crisp right now. Paris, are you conscious?"

"Yeah . . . yeah, conscious. Sure hurts . . ."

"You've got broken ribs. I'll get the first-aid kit in a minute. First I've got to stabilize the containment system, or it's all over. We've got coolant leaks, and we have to keep that sirillium refrigerated. If it goes above two degrees centigrade, it could expand and blow out of the tanks, and be ignited by the other explosions out there. Can you get up? Tom?"

He tried to sit up, but his battered ribs drove pain through his body, and he collapsed again.

B'Elanna shoved a hand under his neck and pushed him upward into a sitting position.

He bent forward and winced, then shifted over onto his knees. "I can't breathe . . ."

"There's a coolant breach," she told him. "I'm hoping the damage control system can lock it down automatically. Till then I guess we'll have to breathe fumes and try to keep from turning green."

"Too late . . . have you looked in a mirror lately?"

"Take the helm, will you? We've got to get control back or we'll be kicked to bits."

"You want me to restart the engines?"

"What difference does it make?" she said. "The sirillium traces out there are already ignited."

"Oh . . . sure." On his hands and knees, his sandy curls dusted with chips of debris, Paris winced his way back toward the helm and crawled into the seat. When he got there, he could barely hold his head up and had to lean against the bulkhead as he picked at the controls with his good hand.

"Restarting impulse drive," he said on a cough.

He punched the ignition, and the shuttle's impulse drive burped and surged, knocking the shuttle forward into a surge, which then knocked it sideways and turned it upside down. The artificial gravity system whined, squawked, and fought to keep sense in the cabin, but not before throwing B'Elanna backward into the opposite bulkhead.

Dazed, she closed her eyes and shook her head, but that only made things worse. Now her spine and shoulders ached on top of her sore knees from being thrown down the first time. She clawed her way back across the tilted deck to the containment controls and kept adjusting and balancing.

The impulse engines kept puffing. B'Elanna heard

them even before Paris shouted back, "I can't get the engines to settle down enough to give me any steering control!"

"Keep trying!" She stumbled forward to the main control panel and tapped the comm console. *"Voyager! Can you read us? Voyager, come in!"*

"Chakotay to shuttlecraft! Can you read us? Lieutenant Carey, boost the gain from the ship to the shuttle."

"Sir, that could agitate the ignited sirillium traces even more."

"Take the chance."

"Aye, sir."

"—craft—Tor—"

Chakotay leaned over the console and shouted, "Torres! We read you! What's your status?"

"Atmosphere leakage . . . coolant disruptions, some injury, and containment tanks . . . in flux—"

"Carey, give it another boost."

"Aye, sir . . . boosting."

"Voyager, can you read?"

"Yes, we read you. Can you hear me now, B'Elanna?"

"I can hear you. Why the fireworks?"

"We had an incident. It's under control. Let's concentrate on getting you back. Are you all right?"

"I'm in one piece."

"What about Paris?"

"He's in about four pieces, but trying to work. We're restarting engines, but not having much luck

with thrust control, and we're getting some impulse cavitation because of the turbulence. Seems like space itself is blowing up around us out here."

Angry with himself for making a perfectly sensible set of choices and somehow having them all turn out deadly, Chakotay instantly thought about sickbay and what was happening down there. Why had Kes gone crazy? Klingons? Val-something? Kes was telepathic in some weird definition of the trait, and it had to have something to do with that meld.

If the meld was affecting Kes without even being in contact with Tuvok, without even being on the same deck with Tuvok, what was it doing to the captain?

He paused and added up the situation. In the shuttlecraft, which was cracking and disabled, he had B'Elanna and Paris. Both had Maquis experience, as he had himself, working as rebels aboard less-than-perfect ships. They could both handle shabby machinery and scary moments, but if they were hurt, how much could he expect of them? And no matter how valiant, they couldn't attitude away a contaminated atmosphere.

"Mr. Kim, as soon as you can get a fix on the shuttlecraft, try to throw the tractor beams on it."

"Trying already, sir, but I can't get a stable fix. If they could move closer to us—"

"Torres, can you move any closer to us?"

There was silence for several seconds.

Then Paris's voice—*"Sir, we've got a little problem with the piloting controls. I'm trying to trim the*

*ship to use the currents, but those are . . . ow . . .
oh . . ."*

Beside Chakotay, Harry Kim winced sympatheti-
cally. "Sounds like he's hurt, sir."

"I know." Chakotay straightened. "Mr. Carey,
take the helm."

Carey looked up, then understood and lunged for
the helm. "Impulse drive ready, Commander."

"Take us forward into the turbulence until Mr.
Kim can get the tractor beam onto the shuttle. You
two coordinate your actions."

"Aye, aye, sir, ahead one-quarter impulse."

"Aye, sir," Kim responded, his face still creased
with worry for their two crewmates.

"Evacuate the ship's outer areas in case there's a
hull rupture—"

"Chakotay! What are you doing?" Torres again.

"We're coming in to throw that net over you," he
said, knowing exactly what she was going to say
back. "We'll get as close to you as we can."

*"That's crazy! These currents'll grab the primary
hull and turn you upside down. Voyager's too massive
to navigate under power through this area. Give us a
chance to power our way out!"*

"I'll give you as long as it takes for us to get to you.
If you can think of something to do, feel free."

*"You'll never get in this deep. We're being dragged
in the wrong direction. Paris and I are done for. We're
replaceable. Don't risk the whole ship."*

"Oh, no, I can't leave you," he told her. "You
serve too important a function on this ship."

"What I do isn't that important! Carey can be chief engineer."

"It's not that," Chakotay continued. "I just need somebody to blame things on. If the two of you are gone, life around here won't be any fun anymore."

"Chakotay, I just got that ship put together after the last hoop we had to jump through. If we live through this, remind me to hurt you later. You better have your spirit guide with you when I get back on board."

"This from a woman who tried to kill her own spirit guide."

"It was ugly."

"Sir—"

"Yes, Tom?"

"When we get back . . . maybe you could introduce me to B'Elanna's spirit guide animal. Bet it'll be a hell of a night out."

"Don't pay any attention to him," B'Elanna said. *"He's delirious."*

Chakotay told her, "Don't overstress your engines. We'll get as close as we can. Just keep yourselves from drifting farther away. This might take a few minutes."

"Acknowledged," B'Elanna's voice crackled back, and immediately after it, Paris's: *"I'll try not to bleed to death."*

This was getting out of hand. Flashes of Paris, flashes of the plateau—

Kathryn Janeway closed her eyes for a moment

and forced herself to concentrate. The *Excelsior*. The bridge. The battle. Valtane.

What had just happened? Why was her mind— Tuvok's mind—shifting gears over and over? What were all those flashes?

She wanted to think they were only erratic non-sensicals, brought on by stress or the eccentricities of melding, but she refused to believe that. A Vulcan's mind was orderly, and these things were out of order. That meant something was happening to Tuvok.

Opening her eyes, she looked at him. He was still crouched over Valtane, but now he appeared startled, as if he'd just been stung by a bee.

"Damage report!"

Captain Sulu appeared through a cloud of electrical smoke, snapping orders and directing his crew to the most critical systems.

"Hull breach on deck twelve." Commander Rand's voice came through the twisting smoke. "Section forty-seven . . . we've lost power on decks five, six, and ten . . . casualty reports are coming in . . . nineteen wounded . . ."

"I saw her again, Tuvok," Janeway said, inching close to her officer and the dead lieutenant. "The girl. As Valtane died just now, it seemed to cause the memory to resurface."

Tuvok seemed not to hear her, or not to care, both of which were significant, though she didn't have a clue what to make of either. Slowly he took the time to lay Valtane on the deck, with a great deal more care and gentleness than she had ever seen in him since.

He looked up, but not at her. Not at anything. He seemed to be looking up at whatever he saw in his own mind.

"What is it?" she asked, determined to prod the situation forward out of this mental quicksand lapping at them.

He stared, then blinked, then his brows drew tight as he tried to make a conclusion. Struggling inside his head, he murmured, "Something has gone wrong with the mind-meld."

Janeway started to ask him to specify, but restrained herself. He would tell her if he knew what was happening. A pointless question might only stress him further, lay more responsibility on him than she wanted him to bear.

She was supposed to be the guide, yet she might as well be leading him through a lightless cave with a smothering odor filling it.

"When Lieutenant Valtane died just now," Tuvok went on, looking down at the body, "I began to feel the anxiety . . . the fear . . . his death seemed to cause the traumatic memory to resurface."

"What are you saying?" she asked. "That you had a memory flash of the girl during his death eighty years ago?"

"No . . . I do not remember its happening back then. However, I do feel a connection between the two memories here and now—in the mind-meld."

"So they *are* related. Then what—"

Suddenly a pair of legs appeared before them.

Janeway looked up to see Captain Sulu standing only a meter away, gaping down at her and Tuvok.

At *her?*

With a surge of shock and even anger, Captain Sulu balled his fists and demanded, "Who the hell are *you?*"

"The needs of the one outweighed the needs of the many."

Captain James Kirk
Star Trek III: The Search for Spock

CHAPTER

15

"PARIS? TOM, ARE YOU CONSCIOUS?"

"Me? I better be. I'm in too much pain to be asleep. That Chakotay . . . you've gotta give him credit, trying to come in after us."

"Credit for craziness," Torres allowed saucily. "The stress on *Voyager*'s hull will exceed safety limits."

She sank into the navigator's seat, because she'd done all she could aft, and the coolant leak was sneaking slowly forward. This was the only good air left, *good* being relative.

"Have any luck?" he asked.

Hating the motion, she shook her head. "None at all. I've pinched and picked and rerouted and reprogrammed."

"Well," he said, then paused for a grip of pain. "Well, maybe Chakotay'll think of something."

"He's not an engineer. It'd be a lot more prudent for him to give up on us. We're being shoved away from *Voyager* ten meters for every two they push through. Even if they loop around the other side, we'll be dead by then."

He gazed out the shuttle's viewport at the oppressive sparkling-blue nebula that was soon to poison and then crush them. Paris looked remarkably clean-cut and vulnerable for a self-professed rebel. He was afraid. B'Elanna could see that.

So was she. This hadn't started out as a life-threatening mission. What had gone so wrong that their own ship fired on them?

Obviously an accident of some kind, but a deadly one. Those things could happen when technology was high-flying and the most complex of physical and theoretical science was held on a very thin tether. She'd nearly lost *Voyager* itself to such things. She forgave, but for the next few minutes, the last of her life, she wouldn't be able to forget.

"I've tried everything I could think of." She sighed. "I don't know what else to do. We're heading in the wrong direction, and there's no way to steer, even if propulsion was on-line. I just don't know what else I can do . . . I guess we're done." Forcing herself to meet his worried eyes, she admitted, "I'm sorry. I can't think of anything else. I'm very sorry."

Paris let his head rest back against the bulkhead beside his useless helm. "What's that supposed to mean? Is this your fault somehow? Tell me how."

"I'm an engineer. I should be able to come up with alternatives. There just aren't any in a situation this simple. There are only so many twists a system can take. A mechanical problem becomes my fault. That's how it is."

"In Starfleet, you mean?"

"I guess that's what I mean." She sank back in her seat, trying to avoid the ceiling as fumes began to gather up there. She came to life for one more instant and threw the scanner into the bulkhead, then settled back again. "I feel like I've fallen through ice and there are a hundred people standing around the hole, but nobody can get to me."

Rubbing his hastily tied arm wound, Paris pondered. "How much fuel do we have?"

"Not much. I had this shuttle only a quarter fueled because it's volatile and I knew we wouldn't need it on the way back. There's hardly any left."

"Uh-huh . . . okay, no fuel. So what else?"

"Five tanks full of sirillium," she said roughly. "You want to make soup and have a last meal?"

Paris stared at the ceiling above Torres's head. "What if we jettisoned the atmosphere?"

She screwed a nasty look through his sweat-glazed brow. "We'd exhale ourselves to death."

He leaned forward with cramping effort. "No, wait—if we vent the atmosphere out the right ducts and turn the shuttlecraft so we're pretty much facing *Voyager,* then blow the sirillium out the back end and ignite it—"

"So we blow off the back end of the sh—" Torres felt as if her brain were exploding, and she stood up so sharply that she thrust her head into the growing cloud of pink poison. "We'd shoot straight out to them! It could work! I thought I'd thought of everything!"

"I thought you had too. Luckily, you have me."

"It'll blow out the back end." She thought aloud, trying to keep her breathing shallow. "Probably buckle the plates . . . and the impact'll probably kill us . . . but it'll punch us forward, *if* we can hold our heading with momentum from the vented atmosphere to rotate us in the right direction. I like this. It'll take me a few minutes to weld the aft plates shut so we'll have a sliver of a chance of surviving—"

Paris nodded. "Ah, optimism."

"You get the vents ready. Can you?"

"I'll try. I mean, of course I can."

She paused and peered out the forward port, though she could see nothing there but flashing sirillium and other chemicals going wild with the phaser reaction. "Maybe we should inform Chakotay."

"Hmmm . . . that's a tough one. We should at least try, shouldn't we?"

"Fine." She leaned forward and keyed the comm system. *"Voyager,* this is Torres. We've got an idea."

She waited for a response, but none came.

"Try another channel," Paris suggested.

"I know." She did, but still nothing came through the static that remotely sounded like a voice. "Communications are down. I can't get through."

"So . . . what do we do?"

"We ignite the tanks and hope *Voyager*'s sensors

are on-line without interference and they can pick us up. Otherwise we'll spin off into the other side of the nebula and they'll never find us in time. Not that it matters. When we blow the sirillium, the impact'll probably kill us anyway."

With effort, Paris turned and wagged a finger. "You said 'probably.'"

"That's what I said." Favoring a knee she suddenly realized was very sore and twitching, Torres limped to the amidships starboard bosun's locker and dug around for what should have been standard equipment—a relatively simple phaser torch used for mending gashes in the inner bulkheads and struts.

"I'll weld the cargo bay shut," she told him, realizing she was just talking to hear her own voice. In her mind she walked Paris through the adjustments to the atmospheric decompressors and the reserve system which would keep them alive when they tapped the mains for thrust. Humidity control would have to be sacrificed—that hardware would be in use for the network cross-feed. The emergency environmental recycling scrubbers were already overloaded with trying to contain the coolant leak. It was about half working. The coolant wasn't filling the cabin, but it wasn't pleasant in there, either. After the tanks were blown, all bets were off. They could suffocate or be poisoned in the ten seconds necessary to propel them forward to *Voyager*.

At least after that, one way or the other, their problem would be all finished.

What happened to the lighting? Torres glanced

around in frustration as she noticed the cloying dimness. Doing close work now, she needed to be able to see, and more than half the lights were out. The salmon-pink emergency lights glowed on the deck, reacting with the pink coolant smoke, casting an unassured rosy glow on half the cabin and shadows on everything else. Though easy on the eyes, the emergency lighting was less friendly than the shadowless artificial daylight ordinarily cast in the shuttle cabin.

This was insane riskiness here. They might as well stick antimatter down their pants and ignite it.

After yanking the amidships double hatches closed, she settled down to do the welding. The outer hatch would probably blow open, but the inner hatch had a slim chance of holding. Most of the blast would be directed outward, especially if she tripped the automatic lock on the aft cargo hatch and let it drift open. If there were no resistance on the other side, maybe they'd have a matchstick's chance in hell of surviving.

Yet the activity of welding the hatch was therapeutic. Much better than sitting in the nav seat and waiting to suffocate. Torres had always feared drowning, and death by poisoned atmosphere was the same thing. Better to go up in a ball of angry flame.

Much better.

"This is really stupid, y'know." Paris coughed from the cockpit. "I mean, I know it was my idea, but then again, most of my ideas are stupid."

"Why are we doing it, then?" Torres held a pair of safety goggles to her eyes and turned the phaser torch up to its highest setting as she welded the main seam of the hatch. If this one did not hold, their trip would be very short.

"I'm not sure." He contemplated, muttering as he worked. "Maybe we're going to give *Voyager* a good story to tell. Like, they were valiant until the end, they didn't give up, they tried everything, they did the last possible desperate maniac's thing to do, they were brave, they were dauntless . . . they were . . . help, I need another adjective."

"Delirious? I'm almost ready. Have you got those conduits redirected?"

"Last one's almost finished."

"We're going to kill ourselves," Torres muttered. "Suicide made easy. I'll tell you one thing, though. We're going to die anyway, and at least if we blow ourselves up trying to get out, *Voyager* won't be tempted anymore to come into this mess and rescue us."

"That's for certain."

"And we could do worse than keep our shipmates from risking themselves to save us. I can take that as motivation."

"Okay." Paris tossed her a thready grin. "I'll take it. One more for the list of call-of-duty heroics. I'm ready when you are, mechanically speaking. I wouldn't give you any guarantees about my fluttering stomach."

"Don't worry," Torres huffed. "In a couple of

minutes your stomach won't know what hit it. All right, I'm just about done. I guess if we survive this, I'm going to have to show you a lot more respect."

He batted his eyelashes at her. "Oh, really?"

"Well . . . for a while, anyway."

"I'll take it."

She fanned the air uselessly—the acrid pink miasma was definitely getting thicker. Just before she sat down in the nav seat, she decided to do something about that.

"Tom, give me one of your socks," she said.

"My sock? B'Elanna, I never knew you cared."

"I don't 'care,' mister. I'm going to stuff it into the coolant leak. Hand it over."

He smiled, but kicked off one boot and reached down to pull off his sock.

When he handed it to her, she sneered. "It's wet! Are you sweating that much?"

"I'd rather be," he told her. "That's the blood running down my arm. Sorry."

Torres peered through the salmon glow and felt terrible about what she'd said. "Sorry . . . I forgot. I'll get the first-aid kit and patch your shoulder before we do this."

"Why don't we do it and get it over with?"

"No. I want to patch you up. Nobody should have to die bleeding."

Paris chuckled. "That makes no sense!"

"Maybe not, but it's probably in a Klingon proverb book somewhere. I'll be right back."

In the aft section, just forward of the cargo bay, the coolant rupture fizzed fitfully, burping pink spray so thick that she had to hold her breath as she stuffed the sock into the crack. The fizzing slowed, but didn't stop.

After only a few seconds, she had to hurry back to the cockpit to get another breath.

"Too porous. It did some good, but it won't hold." She panted, feeling her lungs beginning to constrict with lack of oxygen.

Paris didn't say anything, but only nodded resignedly.

Dropping to one knee, Torres pulled the first-aid kit out from under the nav seat and opened it, then rummaged for one of the five-by-five gauze patches with the flexible aluminum coating on one side. "Here, turn your arm this way."

The gash in the outer side of his upper arm was gory and looked very painful. Until she got a good look at it, she hadn't been giving him enough credit for working through the pain and numbness. His fingers on that hand were trembling visibly, and his face was a knot of discomfort. He clamped his lips as she tore the sleeve open a few more inches and sprayed a clotting agent on the wound.

As she raised the five-by-five, she suddenly paused. "This . . . this has adhesive edges . . ."

Paris blinked. "So?"

"So . . . just a minute!"

She pushed off the deck, and accidentally off his sore arm, but ignored his quick intake of breath and rushed to the coolant rupture. This just might work—shoving the sock as far into the crack as she could without pushing it all the way through, she laid the patch over the top of the sock and pressed her fingers around the adhesive ridges, one side at a time, very carefully, so there were no air bubbles.

The leak sputtered, lifted the last corner of the five-by-five, then went quiet.

She glanced forward. "I think this can work!"

"What?" Paris rasped back.

"I patched the leak with the bandage. Between this and the sock, we might buy ourselves a few more minutes."

She dashed back to the nav seat and sat down, then reached over and strapped Tom tightly into his seat with the safety harness that so rarely, if ever, had been used.

"I'm beginning to think we could just survive this," she said with renewed vigor. "We just might."

"I will if you will," he grunted. Then the pain of broken ribs cut through him, and he pressed his head back against the seat and crammed his eyes closed.

Torres gave him a few seconds to regain control. When he opened his eyes and managed a nod, she reached forward to the control panel. "Ready."

Paris drew a series of short breaths to steady himself, then put his good hand on his own panel. "Ready."

"Go ahead."

Knowing what he had to do, Paris tapped the controls and caused a hissing sound along the sides of the shuttlecraft, on the outer hull. *Sssssst . . . sssssst . . .*

Meter by meter the shuttle wobbled in space,

bobbing on an imaginary surface until the nose began to draw an arch toward a specific point.

"Almost have it . . ." Paris was drenched in sweat now. *"Voyager* thirty degrees off the starboard bow . . . twenty degrees . . ."

"Opening the aft hatch—"

"Ten degrees . . ."

"Blowing the tanks," Torres said tightly. "Hold that heading!"

"Five degrees . . . dead ahead!"

"Ignition!"

PART
THREE

"KHAQQ calling *Itasca*. We must be on you but we cannot see you . . . gas is running low . . . We are on the line of position 157 degrees — 337 degrees — we will repeat this message on 6210 kilocycles, wait listening on 6210 kilocycles — we are running north and south."

Last messages received by the
Coast Guard Cutter *Itasca*
from Amelia Earhart, July 1937

CHAPTER
16

"INTRUDER ALERT! GET SECURITY UP HERE!"

Well, that was about as excited as Janeway had seen Captain Sulu yet.

Given the intruder alert, she had a second or two of leeway. She used it to lean toward Tuvok.

"What's happening?" she asked. "They're reacting to me. Why can they see me?"

"Yes, I am aware of the change in the telepathic connection between us. Suddenly you have become part of this memory, Captain. I remember your being here."

"What? Is it something the Doctor's doing?"

"I am uncertain. I would have to break the meld in order to regain—"

"No. Don't. I think we're getting close to something. It all centers on the death of Valtane."

By ignoring Captain Sulu, they only angered him. He crowded her and Tuvok.

"I asked you a question!" he snapped to Janeway. "Who are you, and what are you doing on my ship?"

Tuvok glanced up at him, then ignored him again and looked at his—well, his other captain.

"It is an indication that the rate of deterioration in my brain has increased. At advanced stages of a *t'lokan* schism, memories and thought processes become distorted and confused."

"Ensign," Sulu demanded of Tuvok, "do you know this woman?"

"Direct hit!" Commander Rand shot from her position. "On the port bow! Shields down to twenty percent!"

Sulu glanced between Rand and Janeway, and made his choice. He rushed to a console. "I'll reroute the auxiliary power to structural integrity."

Another jolt hit the ship—a hard one.

"Maybe something happened in this moment between the two of you," Janeway pressed on to Tuvok. "Some detail you aren't remembering. I want you to try replaying those events one more time."

Tuvok appeared troubled at the idea of having to go through Valtane's death all over again. "I will try, but I must point out that if my neural structure collapses while we're still in the meld, you will suffer brain damage as well."

"I understand," she said, even though she didn't. Forward movement was forward movement.

Sulu finished what he was doing, and turned back

to them instantly. "All right, let's have it. Who are you? Is that a Starfleet uniform?"

Janeway stood up to face him. She felt a little silly talking to a memory. It was like trying to direct a dream. "Captain, I don't have time to explain to you, but I'm a Starfleet officer. I've been working undercover in this sector for a year. The mission is highly classified and very sensitive, but—"

"Not sensitive enough to have someone I don't know on my ship," Sulu said.

"Captain, the Klingons are closing to two thousand kilometers!" the helsman quacked.

"Hard port, heading two seven zero mark zero six!"

"Two seven zero mark zero six, aye!"

"Captain," Tuvok attempted, "you must trust us both. She is not a threat. You have my word—"

"Ensign, do you know this woman?"

"I do, sir."

"Then I suggest you start explaining before I throw *both* of you in the brig."

Janeway stepped forward, vowing to keep control over the situation and Tuvok's mind on its course. "Captain, are you aware of anything in Ensign Tuvok's service record that would suggest he suffered a traumatic experience involving the death of a young girl?"

Captain Sulu's rock-etching eyes widened at the sudden change of subject. "I beg your pardon?"

"When Tuvok was a boy, he let a girl fall from a precipice. He's been repressing the memory and—"

"Engineering to the captain!"

"Sulu here."

"We've got a warp core overload! We may have to eject the core—"

"Stand by, engineering. Helm, drop out of warp."

"Dropping out of warp, sir."

The aft turbolift doors gushed open, and four security guards piled out.

Sulu pointed at Janeway and Tuvok. "Take those two to the brig."

The guards didn't even stop moving. They engulfed Janeway and Tuvok, and if this was a dream or an illusion, it sure had a hell of a grip.

And bad breath.

"Tuvok!" Janeway called.

Tuvok shook off one of the two guards grappling with him, and closed his eyes, fighting on two fronts.

Plink—crew quarters. Again.

Tuvok and the scent of tea, Valtane and other juniors milling about.

Again. This was getting to look like a crazy quilt. The same patches, all in different patterns.

Could they still see her? Janeway moved to Tuvok's side, using his body as a shield from the other young officers, all of whom were involved in their own personal business, luckily.

She kept her voice way, way down.

"Everything is centered on the same sequence of events. The repressed memory must have some connection to one of these moments."

"The question is," Tuvok agreed, "which moment?" He picked up an herb and was about to drop it into the tea, then changed his mind and picked up a different herb.

As if it mattered!

"The bridge seems to be the place," Janeway suggested. "It has to be the bridge. We keep returning to the battle with the Klingons."

"That is correct. And there does seem to be a special emphasis on the death of Lieutenant Valtane." Tuvok said it, then glanced across the quarters at Valtane, as if worried he might've said that too loudly.

"Yes," Janeway agreed. "We do seem to be drawn to that event. Maybe something happened in that moment between the two of you. Maybe he said something or did something that you've repressed. Something you don't want to remember."

Tuvok frowned. "I do not know what that would be. He was dead by the time I reached him. At least . . . I believe he was."

"Maybe there's more to what happened in that moment," Janeway insisted. "The only way to be sure is to return and pay close attention this time. Except that now your memories are starting to react to my presence. It would be best if Captain Sulu didn't notice me on the bridge."

"Attention on deck!" somebody snapped.

Commander Rand had just entered the quarters. "How are you this fine morning, Ensign?" the woman asked, moving to Tuvok.

"I am well, Commander," Tuvok answered. "Thank you."

"I thought you might like to see some of this morning's comm traffic." Rand handed him a PADD. "There's a message from the *Yorktown* I thought you might be—who are you?"

She was looking at Janeway. Surprise, surprise.

Tuvok sighed in almost human frustration. "She is a friend of mine. Captain Janeway."

Janeway forced up a smile. "Nice to meet you, Commander."

"New uniform, Captain?" Rand asked.

"Something I'm trying out."

"Hmm . . ." Rand looked at her another second, then said, "Excuse me," and turned to her young officers. "All right, gamma shift! It's time to defend the Federation against gaseous anomalies!"

The other juniors started heading for the door in a squeamish replay of what Janeway had seen before.

"May I have a word with you, Commander?" Tuvok asked just as Rand was about to leave.

The woman turned back. "What is it, Ensign?"

"I thought you should know you have a spot of lubricant on your uniform jacket."

Rand looked down at her jacket. "Really— where?"

"Here." Tuvok lithely raised his hand and clawed Rand's neck in a Vulcan nerve pinch.

Her head snapped back, and she fell like a sandbag. What a talent.

Janeway knelt beside the woman. "You could've just asked her," she said, eyeing Tuvok.

He knelt there too, and together they started

pulling off Rand's jacket. "It's been my experience that asking female officers to remove their clothing could lead to a misunderstanding."

"Mr. Chakotay, there's been an explosion inside the nebula!"

Not five seconds later, *Voyager* was buffeted by a residual pressure wave from directly forward, and the whole ship physically wobbled and dipped slightly to starboard.

Chakotay rode out the wave, then hurried to the tactical monitor on the helm and tried to decipher what had happened.

From the intensity reading on the scale, he couldn't clearly tell whether that explosion was natural or otherwise.

"Was it the shuttlecraft?" he asked. "Did they self-destruct?"

Lieutenant Carey bent over his sensors and said, "Detecting some debris . . . bits and pieces of hard material in the nebula—but, sir, it doesn't read like enough mass for a whole shuttlecraft."

"Check your readings. Make sure of that."

"Checking, sir."

"Mr. Kim, have you got anything?"

"I think," Kim began, peering unhappily into his readouts, "I'm picking up a single detonation of severe power. But it's not ignited fuel. It's a surge of ignited sirillium."

Chakotay came to the edge of the lower bridge and quietly asked, "The sirillium tanks?"

Kim looked down mournfully. "I think I have to conclude that, sir."

Saddened, baffled, and angry, Chakotay gazed at the deck for a moment. He felt the eyes of the bridge crew after a pause, and realized what he had to do.

"Prepare to bring the ship about," he said, his voice rough. "Mr. Carey, take the helm."

The lieutenant looked at him for a moment, then dully answered, "Yes, sir."

The passive twitter of bridge mechanicals gave Chakotay and the others no comfort, as the ship shifted from forward thrusters to reverse thrusters. They wouldn't bother to turn around, but just rumble backward against the hostile nebula until they were out of it.

After this, they wouldn't even have any sirillium to collect. Not even that. Not the smallest profit.

A complete waste of time and lives, all because of one ill-timed phaser shot.

Chakotay dumped himself into the command seat and felt as if he were sinking deeper and deeper into the leather, falling endlessly through the decks.

He'd lost them.

A simple, not particularly important mission had cost the ship its chief engineer and its primary pilot, not to mention two people the rest of the crew had learned to trust.

What would the captain say?

"Back us out of here, Mr. Carey," he said after enough time had passed to shift the necessary systems. "After I've informed the captain, I'll address the crew."

Carey didn't respond, though he should have.

In fact, no one said anything. The silence was biting.

The bridge sounds bleeped and whirred as if to whistle back their lost shipmates.

"Mr. Kim," he said soggily, "advise the crew to stabilize all stations after we leave the nebula, and all department heads report back to Mr. Carey on the ship's condition and damage, if any."

In his periphery he saw Kim nod, but the ensign also made no verbal response.

Suddenly Carey bent over his sensor grid and then bent a little farther. "Sir . . ."

"Something, Lieutenant?"

"I . . ."

Chakotay shot out of his chair and never even touched the deck as he rushed to the helm. "Something?"

"I'm picking up a . . . solid . . ." Carey paused and fine-tuned his controls, unsatisfied. "It's acting like a . . . meteor."

"Mr. Kim! Analyze mass and content of Mr. Carey's projectile. Is it natural?"

Kim worked his board. "Size is roughly ten meters . . . mass . . . sir, the mass is only four metric tons! It's hollow! Can't be a natural object! It's got to be the shuttle with a blown cargo bay!"

"Engage tractor beam! Bring it alongside!"

The bridge crew took a collective breath and held it.

Chakotay swung back to the helm. "Mr. Carey, continue confirmation procedure."

"Yes, sir. Sir, it's not a natural object. It's trailing traces of chemical eruption. They must've blown the sirillium tanks and struck a match. They're coming toward us at an angle of point-five degrees."

"Use the tractors to adjust that. Don't let them slip past us, or we'll lose them."

Harry Kim swallowed hard. "That detonation was extremely concentrated, sir. The concussion must've punched right through the forward cabin. I don't think . . . I don't think there's going to be much to retrieve."

"They got themselves this far," Chakotay said. "We'll bring them in the rest of the way and take what we get."

Carey turned. "If I were Torres, I'd have welded the inner cargo doors shut. Maybe she did that."

"I hope so." Chakotay fought to keep any anxiety or anticipation out of his voice, just in case the results were no better than Kim expected.

They all peered at the harsh blue soup on the forward screen, and in a few moments could see the form of the cargo shuttle streaking toward them. Meteor—yes, it was coming toward them as if hit in the back end by a meteor. That's just about what it must have felt like, if they ignited on-board sirillium tanks.

"Keep those tractors ready, Mr. Carey. Don't let the readings fool you. Do it visually as much as you can."

"I intend to, sir."

"Sorry," Chakotay offered. Leaving behind his desires to direct the details, he crossed the bridge to the upper deck and leaned over Kim's controls. "Mr. Kim? How're we doing?"

"Sir, in this turbulent inward current, I don't think we could bring the shuttle all the way around to the main bay. Not safely, anyway."

"You have another suggestion? The docking ports on the secondary hull, I'll bet."

"Yes, sir, and given the pattern of this current," Harry said, pausing for a moment to look at his screen, "I'd recommend the . . . port side."

"Okay, you're with me. Mr. Carey, you have the bridge."

"Aye, aye, sir."

"Bring that shuttle around to docking port four."

"Aye, sir. I'll try to have it there by the time you arrive."

"That would be above and beyond the call of duty, and now, of course, I'm holding you to it."

Carey tossed him a hopeful glance as he took the tactical post. "Easy for me to take credit, sir, when Harry did most of the——"

The lift doors closed on the end of Carey's sentence.

Riding the turbolift down to the secondary hull, Chakotay could almost swear he felt the *clunk* as the shuttle bumped up against the docking port and pressure was equalized. He knew he couldn't really feel it—in fact, the timing was wrong. The shuttle wouldn't even be alongside yet. But he kept imagining it over and over.

He looked at Harry Kim. "Worried?"

Kim's youthful face was stiff, but his eyes were tightly betraying what he was thinking. There really wasn't any right answer. If he was worried, that said he was concerned about his friends, but it also meant his confidence in the ship and the rescue methods was less than it should be.

"Tom and B'Elanna can handle an emergency, sir," he said ultimately, choosing his words very carefully. "But they didn't expect to be under fire. They didn't even have the shuttle's shields up."

"Why not?"

"The shields would've constantly tried to repel the energy currents. It would've been a much rougher ride, sir."

"Shields down . . . B'Elanna said she had a coolant leak in the cabin. If she didn't manage to get it locked down, we're not going to very much enjoy what we find when we open up that hatch."

"Sir," Kim said then, "what do you think happened to Kes? Why did she start firing the phasers? And what was all that about Klingons?"

"I don't know. But I intend to find out."

Finally the lift pressed to a stop and the doors flew open. Chakotay led the run down two corridors and through the small-engine maintenance bay to the docking port. Immediately he checked the panel.

"Docked," he said. "But not equalized yet. Another few seconds . . ."

Harry Kim stood on the other side of the entranceway, his arms at his sides as he tried not to make any overt gestures that would give away his tension, but it was almost palpable.

Seconds were long and tedious until finally the green light flashed: EQUALIZED.

The hatch hissed, and Kim lunged to open it, giving up on trying to appear unconcerned.

Putrid, acidic atmosphere gushed out at them and almost drove them back. Chakotay had to step back to suck a clean breath and hold it long enough to reach inside through the pink pall.

Instantly the sound of coughing led him and Kim to the two crewmen. Chakotay found B'Elanna first—she was trying to haul Paris out.

He waited until Kim grappled with Paris, then he dragged B'Elanna out and struggled with her about halfway down the corridor, into the fresh air. There he lowered her to sit on the deck and hurried back to help with Paris, who was barely walking.

"I'm surprised you two are alive," Chakotay commented. "Pretty nasty in there, but you locked down the leak. How'd you do it?"

"Funny thing," Paris choked out. "With all our technology . . . we couldn't come up with anything better than . . . stuffing a sock into a hole."

He winced and choked, his head heavy and breathing labored as they lowered him to the deck under the whirring vents. Sure enough, one of his boots and one sock were missing.

"That's porous," Kim said. "How'd you—"

"We patched it with a sterile bandage," B'Elanna rasped, her voice craggy from the irritation of a contaminated atmosphere. "I was going to bandage his arm, and bandaged the coolant instead."

As Harry held Paris up in a sitting position so he could breathe easier, Chakotay checked for bleeding.

"Not a very attractive wound on your arm."

"I hope it leaves a scar." Paris gasped fitfully, "Girls like scars."

"We can arrange for the doctor to leave you a scar. What else, Tom?"

"Ribs . . . terrible, shattered, smashed . . . never be the same . . ."

Kim smiled, mostly with relief. "Don't worry. You'll fuse. I think it's all an act. You're really made of rubber."

B'Elanna pointed at Paris and started to speak, but was clutched by a fit of coughing and slumped back against the wall, her face cramped with frustration at not getting a barb in when she had a chance.

Chakotay said, "Harry, let's get these two to sickbay before we get into a conversation we'll all regret."

"What's the prognosis? How are they?"

Chakotay faced the Doctor in an anteroom of sickbay, around the corner from where Tuvok and the captain were still locked in their mind-meld. The Doctor, being a holograph, had no problem monitoring both situations through the ship's computer, so they decided to keep Paris and B'Elanna away from the captain, to minimize any disturbance.

All they needed was another disturbance.

"Lieutenant Torres has some first- and second-degree burns on her hands and legs," the Doctor said. "She's bruised and has a pulled ligament in her left leg. Mr. Paris is more severely injured, with some spinal trauma, seven fractured ribs, and an open gash on his upper arm. However, I can fuse the bones and close the wound rather easily. The ligament and the bruises will take longer. Some things simply have to rebound on their own. They both have lung damage from inhaling the coolant and other contaminants, but that too can be cured. They'll both be sore for a few days, but the prognosis is good. I would say they were both most fortunate."

"Good." Chakotay folded his arms in a deliberately imposing manner. "Now that we have those two taken care of, Doctor, is there something I should know about Kes?"

With a contemplative pause, the Doctor admitted, "Yes, there is."

"Well?"

"Kes requested that I not inform you of her condition."

He tried to step away, but Chakotay moved in front of him—as if that would matter if a holographic display really wanted to get around him. "Kes came onto the bridge and started firing the phasers at 'Klingons.' The phaser fire ignited the trace sirillium left in that part of the nebula and almost killed Torres and Paris."

Obviously troubled, the Doctor worked through the problem for several seconds.

"I'm very sorry," he said. "Perhaps Neelix can shed some light on the situation."

Chakotay leaned into the ward and quietly called, "Neelix."

The Talaxian looked up, spotted Chakotay in the anteroom, patted B'Elanna on the shoulder, kissed Kes, and crossed the ward into the smaller area.

He was immediately faced off by a not particularly accommodating first officer.

Chakotay pulled him into a place where they couldn't be seen. "All right, Neelix, what's going on with Kes?"

The worried Talaxian glanced back into the other part of sickbay, where Kes was hovering over their two injured crewmates, applying burn treatment to B'Elanna's right hand.

"I can't . . . I can't tell you," Neelix attempted. "I swore an oath to Kes not to tell. She made me promise. She doesn't want anything to interfere with the captain's effort to help Mr. Vulcan, and I have to . . . well, I *have* to."

"Maybe, but when she's up on the bridge and firing the phasers, the whole story changes, doesn't it? As acting captain, I order you to fill me in."

Neelix wrung his hands and hung his head. He wouldn't look up. "Ask the Doctor."

Chakotay pushed him back against a console and leaned right into his face. "I did. He won't talk. His neck I can't wring, but *yours* . . ."

Maybe Chakotay's jaw was out an inch more than usual, or there were spikes coming out of his eyes, but Neelix buckled.

"All right . . . I'll tell the Doctor to explain it to

you. As Kes's next of kin, I'm authorized to do that."

Chakotay pushed off the console and stuck his head back out into the ward. "Doctor, come in here, please."

The Doctor gave Kes some orders that Chakotay and Neelix couldn't hear, then strode through to where Chakotay and Neelix stood almost in a storage closet.

Instantly Chakotay faced him down. "I tried to keep away from here and not get involved, but now I'm compelled to participate. This mind-meld business is endangering the ship. It's time for you to tell me what's going on, Doctor."

The Doctor looked dubiously at Neelix. "The commander has a point. May I?"

Neelix waved his hands. "I think you'd better. Just do it—you know—quietly."

Hesitating for a moment, the Doctor searched for a way to explain the unexplainable. "Yes, I suppose so. This is something very complicated and unscientific, but Kes is, at times, in contact with Tuvok's mind somehow. She seems to be experiencing flashes of Tuvok's memory, and sometimes even participating in the scenario as a character or some other extension of the vision. But not being a Vulcan, she doesn't have Tuvok's control. And she's not under the shackling influence of the meld, as the captain is."

He held a hand out toward Kes, who at the moment looked perfectly fine and normal, sort of like a poison flower.

Chakotay asked in an annoyed tone, "Why isn't she affected right now? They're still involved in that meld, aren't they?"

The Doctor's brows went up and down a couple of times. "I haven't figured that out yet."

"Well, you're going to have to figure it out. It's affecting the safety of the ship and crew. It almost—" He paused, looked at Kes, and lowered his voice. "It almost killed Paris and Torres."

"Kes is not responsible for that, Mr. Chakotay. You must know that."

"I know she isn't, but I still need to understand it. Make me understand, Doctor."

"At the moment, I don't understand myself. All I can tell you is that Kes is sometimes, not all the time, in contact with Commander Tuvok's telepathic mind, and this elicits an irrational response to some things, such as B'Elanna's Klingon background. Tuvok's Vulcan mind is degrading, and this is causing an aberration in his telepathic senses. His mind is . . . supercharged. I have no way of judging what its limits are, but I can tell you it's dangerous to Kes."

Neelix pushed forward and took Chakotay's arm. "It's going to kill her, Mr. Chakotay!"

Chakotay motioned him to be quiet, and continued facing the Doctor. "Dangerous how?"

"The degradation of Tuvok's mind is advancing. The captain's mental condition is matching his and could collapse if his does. And if the dementia becomes stronger or more persistent, the shock of an imaginary incident could actually cause Kes to die."

Neelix's expression became even more emotional than usual. He grasped Chakotay's arm. "We can't let that happen! We're all hanging on the edge of that cliff. When Tuvok falls, should the captain and Kes and maybe all of us be dragged over the side with him?"

Chakotay stared at him. "What are you saying, Neelix?"

"I'm saying what neither of you has the courage to say! If necessary we should . . . terminate Mr. Tuvok. After all, everything the Doctor has found out says that he's doomed anyway. There . . . I said it."

"Neelix," the Doctor uttered, "this isn't like you at all."

The Talaxian's face flushed mustard yellow. "What would Tuvok say? He would say he has no right to endanger Kes! She's the only one who didn't go into this willingly. If he knew, he would cut the line himself!" He turned again to Chakotay. "Please—please override the Doctor's ethical program and let Tuvok die a dignified death. Would he want to live if his brain were damaged? Should the captain and Kes have to be damaged or killed too? Please, Mr. Chakotay! Don't allow a terrible accident to become an irreversible tragedy!"

Chakotay turned cold all over. Did he have the right to let Tuvok die? Or make Tuvok die? If the situation was crumbling, did the captain's previous orders stand or not?

He gnashed with the problem—this wasn't nice,

safe Federation space where he had multiple layers of medical and command regulations and advice to fall back upon, where things couldn't happen in a vacuum, and where there was always a replacement for lost personnel. These people all depended upon each other far too much to sacrifice one, two, or three casually.

Now their captain, their chief of security, and their only medical assistant were at severe risk. Neelix was right—obligation and loyalty were both strained here. If Tuvok knew what was happening, he'd put an end to it. But could Chakotay make that choice?

"What if we tell the captain about this?" he asked. "Can we communicate with her while she's in the meld?"

"I haven't attempted that," the Doctor said. "There may be some way. I would have to research that. Of course, if the captain knows, then Mr. Tuvok will know. And I have to warn you—any added stress on his mind could overload his mental circuits. He could go into irreversible dementia and take the captain and Kes with him."

Chakotay sank sideways and leaned against the doorway of the storage closet, exhausted with the weight of his responsibility. There went the whole idea of telling the captain. He couldn't get out of this so easily.

Terminate Tuvok . . . not a nice term for an equally not-nice concept.

It could be done, certainly. Those choices had to

be made every day in medical science, in a million hospitals and nursing facilities on thousands of planets.

"The captain is still alive," he said. "I'm not sure I have this kind of authority."

"You have it!" Neelix said frothily. "You have to consider yourself in command until the end of this mission, even if the mission is in the mind! Mr. Tuvok told me that once himself! Isn't that right?"

With an aching sigh, Chakotay nodded. "I guess it's right. Doctor, can you stop the meld without killing Tuvok?"

The Doctor seemed perplexed, even troubled by that. "Terminating the meld artificially could be as dangerous to them as letting them stay in it. I have no way to be sure. This isn't what one would call an exact science."

"I think you should try. No, let me put it differently—I order you to try. If this is risking the captain and Kes too, then we should put a stop to it and try to find some other solution to Tuvok's problem. How soon can you attempt to stop it?"

"Preparations may take a while. There's a delicate balance between—"

"I'm going back to the bridge to think about what Neelix just said. I don't like it, but it's my job to think about it. Keep me posted."

"All right, I've programmed a cortical stimulator to emit thoron radiation. We'll bombard his telepathic cortex. It should be enough to safely terminate the meld."

The Doctor spoke with confidence, but his expression was one of concerned doubt.

Kes wondered if their ship's doctor were in fact capable of so much living worry. There had to be more to this vessel's holographic science than just the illusion of life, for she couldn't think of him as anything less than very alive. She liked him, and she didn't believe she could like something that wasn't real.

But even if Commander Chakotay ordered the meld stopped, how could either he or the Doctor know what the captain wanted? If the brain patterns were activated and something was happening, how could they know what was occurring? Perhaps the captain was closing in on the problem, and things were becoming tense. Maybe that was why Kes herself had been drenched with the meld activity from time to time.

Was it right to bring them out of the meld, only to plunge them back into the unsolved problem all over again?

Still, she understood all the technicals, but these kinds of decisions were mysterious to her. How did these people in charge know what was the right thing to do? Many times she'd seen the captain make decisions without knowing all the facts, without being sure how things would turn out. How did that happen?

On the monitors, the captain's and Commander Tuvok's brain patterns were virtually identical now. Though the patterns had settled down somewhat and the cortical monitors were no longer chirping in electrical panic, there was something quite disturbing about the like nature of those two brain patterns. How could they have merged so much? These two people were of two separate species. Their brains could no more be alike than—

"Begin a twenty-kilodyne burst," the Doctor ordered. "Five-second duration. On my mark . . . now."

Kes had barely made it to the console in order to carry out the directions on his mark.

The device on Tuvok's head lit up with a faint whine of energy, but this time very steady and controlled.

"It's working," the Doctor said. "Their neural patterns are starting to separate."

The main diagnostic console leaped to life with a particularly nerve-shattering alarm. The Doctor calmly checked the readings, as if he didn't believe what he was seeing. Kes waited—was there a malfunction?

"My God . . ." The Doctor looked, tapped the controls, looked again, and was even more confused.

"What is it?" Kes was prompted to ask.

"That's Tuvok's memory engram," the Doctor said, pointing at the monitor, "and that one is the captain's . . . but whose is *this* one?"

CHAPTER
17

CAPTAIN JANEWAY OPENED HER EYES AND THOUGHT THE meld had been broken.

So why was she standing in *Voyager*'s auxiliary engineering area, where the younger officers were trained on specific equipment and simulators?

She and Tuvok had been in sickbay. She looked around. Where was he?

Oh—there.

In a nearby shadow cast by one of the tall reactant injection tanks.

At a training console, looking at a graph of—what was that? Oh—a warp speed to power ratio graph. The woman wasn't dressed in a Starfleet uniform, but instead wore a simple khaki cotton shirt and olive-green trousers, and a brightly patterned paisley silk scarf. On the deck beside her was a short brown leather jacket. Her hair was short and brown, somewhat tousled, and she was on the thin side.

For a moment Janeway didn't recognize her.

But then B'Elanna Torres strode forcefully in from the forward section and impolitely demanded, "Well? Are you ready to try again?"

The woman pivoted around to her in the chair. "No! I'm not ready to try again! How many times do I have to fail at this?"

Torres held out an unappeasing hand. "Look, you're here because Captain Janeway told me to train you to the helm. It's not my fault or anybody else's if you just aren't up to absorbing the details."

"I never saw so many details! Where I come from, there's up and there's down! There's a directional beacon and long-distance equipment and a radio! Speed is something you can stick your hand out and feel. You can't go through 'time-space' with warp engine whatchamacallits! Our aircraft have a front and a back and propellers, and that is the limit!"

"Look," Torres fumed, "I'm trying to help you understand non-Newtonian physics and the cumulative force of warp field energy, but I guess you're just too spoiled to learn!"

"Spoiled? *Spoiled?* Do you know, do you have any idea, who you're speaking to?"

"Yes! A spoiled brat who can't learn the difference between a dilithium crystal and the rock she calls a head!"

Tuvok moved fluidly to Janeway's side and kept himself from being heard—just in case.

"Miss Earhart," he proclaimed quietly.

"But we left her on that planet," Janeway recalled, whispering—as if that really mattered. "The planet where we found the other people who'd been taken from Earth in 1937. She decided to stay!"

Tuvok puzzled briefly, then suggested, "Perhaps this is a memory, or phantom memory, from before we left that planet, Captain. This is what I feared."

"What?"

"An apparently advanced degradation of my mental processes. My mind can no longer distinguish between my own memories and yours, or even what happened and what did not. Since between the two of us, you were the one most affected by Miss Earhart's rediscovery, I believe we are in your mind, Captain."

"*My* mind . . . but, Tuvok, this memory isn't real. This never happened. I never ordered Torres to train her. Amelia Earhart never attempted to learn the helm duties of *Voyager.*"

He looked at her, and for the first time during this venture into the quilted land of thought, attention shifted from him to her.

"Perhaps you believe that she should have," he said.

Janeway watched Torres and Amelia Earhart arguing for a moment, and allowed herself to quit thinking about the complexities of a mind-meld, the condition of Tuvok's deteriorating mind, and the trouble they were in.

Instead, she let herself remember that strange time when a handful of people from 1937 on Earth were discovered held in cryostasis on a planet way over in the Delta Quadrant. How ironic it had been to have the myths of alien abduction actually proven at the same time as the mystery of Earhart's vanishing was solved.

"Yes," she thought aloud. "I've often felt bad about leaving her behind. I had a chance to urge Amelia Earhart to go into space with us, maybe see some of what she had pioneered for women—for everybody . . . and instead I never even tried to talk her into coming along. I've wondered why somebody with enough adventurous spirit to buck the decorum of her own time would choose to stay on some planet instead of soaring out into more adventure."

Tuvok apparently accepted that as—well, logical. "This could very well be your mind trying to satisfy those frustrations."

"Or guilts," Janeway pointed out. She understood emotion better than he did, and she knew darned well what was driving this phantom memory.

The mind-meld was losing its grip, shifting from his memories to hers, and not even real ones. How would they even know for sure if they were in or out of the meld?

"Well," she bridged, "what do you suggest?"

"Since your mind seems to be in control, you will have to be the one to bring us out of the meld."

She looked at him. "How?"

"Concentrate. Think about sickbay and getting back to it."

"Getting back to it?" She held her hand toward

the turbolift door across the engineering bay. "We could walk right over to it here and now. How would we know we were really there?"

"Captain . . ." Tuvok wavered, annoyed by the simplicity of her questions, yet he seemed not to have any answers. "Close your eyes and blot out what you see. Think about the Doctor, sickbay, Kes, and our immediate problems. I can give you no more specific directions. A mind-meld does not possess a nav chart."

"All right, all right. I'll try."

Despite engulfing doubts, she closed her eyes.

After a few moments of aggravation, she opened them again, only to find herself still looking at Amelia Earhart and B'Elanna Torres arguing over the warp graph.

"I can't do it," she said to Tuvok. "I don't know how." She looked up at him. "Now what?"

Glancing at the two other women, then back to her, he seemed genuinely confused. "Perhaps . . . play the scenario through. Once your mind releases its latent frustrations, the meld may automatically relax."

As if given permission to concentrate on the thing she was really interested in, Janeway let herself think about the woman sitting at the graph and a wish that was only now beginning to resurface.

Strange—she thought she had let that one go.

"It was her decision," Janeway contemplated, "but I guess I wasn't satisfied with that. I did for a long time think about her and wish she'd come. And I wondered why she didn't."

Tuvok made a small gesture in that direction. "Why not ask her, Captain?"

As an actor retreats into the theater wings, he stepped backward into the shadow again, as if to release her from concerns about him and give her a chance to follow her own lead.

With a last glance at him, she stiffened and stepped out into the open training area and crossed tentatively toward B'Elanna and Amelia Earhart.

Would they even see her? Would this be like the first moments on *Excelsior?*

Then B'Elanna looked up. "Oh, Captain. I didn't know you were down here."

"Yes, I am. What's the problem?"

Amelia Earhart turned to her, stark features and square jaw patched by the subdued lighting in this cubicle.

"What do you mean, what's the problem? You know what the problem is! Why did you ever bring me on this ship?" Bitterness roiled in the legendary woman's thready voice as she stood up and paced. "I've seldom felt so useless in my life! I hate this ship. I hate you. What have you done to me? What shall I have to do here? Clean the floors? I wish I had died in the Pacific Ocean like I was supposed to!"

In this light her cheekbones shone and her eyes were reduced to wedges. Her short-cropped hair was a sandy tuft, and she seemed rather mannish in her behavior.

Janeway motioned back to the swivel stools at the console. "Sit down, Miss Earhart."

To be more inviting, she sat down herself first.

With her hands on her hips and her head hanging a little, Amelia Earhart stared at the deck, then peered at Janeway.

After a moment she came back and sat down, gripping the sides of the stool with her hands. She stared at her knees. "I'm hopelessly out of date. I fail to understand the simplest details about this vessel. I barely can conceive of why it can go in space, not to begin mentioning how it propels itself without even air to pull on."

Watching the other woman for even the smallest nuance, Janeway asked, "Why . . . did you fly?"

"Because I was told I couldn't."

The answer came so quick as to be rather a shock. Obviously she'd been asked this before.

"I enjoyed flying at first," she went on then. "But even more I enjoyed the adventure, and more than that the limelight. Being famous was like being just a little drunk all the time. I got a lot of things out of the *idea* of flying, and out of *having* flown. I would make one flight, and sustain the fame for years. Speaking engagements, dinners with royalty, cables from presidents, people paying attention to me . . . I was appointed assistant to the general traffic manager at Transcontinental Air Transport. I was supposed to attract 'lady passengers.'"

"Yes, I know," Janeway said. "Later that company became TWA. Very famous, and long-lived."

Amelia looked at her. "How do you know that?"

"I read a few files about your life after you . . . were found."

The aviatrix bobbed her head in a kind of modest

nod. "That's very nice of you." She glanced at the warp graph display one more time, then turned her back on it. "In order to fly across the Atlantic, I had to learn the art of instrumentational flying, and even very few men knew how to do that well. Or at all. But I did it, in 1932. I was off course. I landed in Londonderry, and I had to ask a man in a pasture where I was. After a while, the question of a round-the-world flight came up. I was feeling rather pressured to accomplish this one more thing. I thought I had one more good flight in my system, but when I finished that job I intended to give up long-distance 'stunt' flying."

Leaning forward a little, Janeway clasped her hands and rested her elbows on her knees. "That round-the-world flight . . . beautiful, I'll bet. Exotic places—"

"Quite exotic, yes, very. Miami, San Juan, Africa, Karachi, Calcutta . . . oh, Rangoon, Singapore, Bandoeng . . . the monsoons stopped us in Bandoeng for several days. And I was ill. We were flying a Lockheed Electra 10E. Have you ever seen one?"

Not figuring this was the moment to mention museums and outdated relics, Janeway simply said, "No, I haven't."

"You know, we attempted that flight in 1935. But I wrecked the plane. Taking off from Luke Field in the Pearl Harbor area, I overcompensated for a low right wing and we swung out of control. The undercarriage collapsed against the runway. Luck was with us—there was no fire—but the damage required shipping the plane back to California. We couldn't make another attempt for nearly two years. Did you know, when we finally tried again, as we left Bandoeng we took the parachutes off the plane and shipped them home? After all, what good did we imagine they would be over the Pacific?"

Janeway glanced over at Tuvok in the shadow and muttered, "I guess I'd have to know it, or this wouldn't be happening, could it?"

Amelia looked up, confused. "Pardon me?"

"Oh, nothing, nothing. Miss Earhart, I'm sorry if this is stressful for you. I suppose I thought you might enjoy being part of a whole new kind of adventure, the legacy of the kind of flights you embarked upon. I didn't mean to overwhelm you."

"It's not your fault," Amelia said. "I've had to look at myself in rather a new light. I finally have to admit that I was a wonderful show woman, but maybe . . . it may be that I wasn't a good enough pilot. I knew how to make the plane fly and how to find my way most places, but the actual science behind flight was something I mostly ignored." She tipped her head toward the warp graph. "What Miss Torres calls the 'physics.' I learned 'enough' but never 'all.' I should've been able to find the cutter *Itasca*'s directional beacon. We weren't that far from Howland Island, but we just simply could not find it. I supposed that wanting to have done things and knowing how to do them well . . . seem not to be the same."

"Is that what you think is important about Amelia Earhart?" Janeway asked. "Whether or not you were a good pilot?"

The other woman looked up. "Isn't it?"

"Not to me. Not to the millions of women who came after you, fighting into the wind because of you. You were more than a pilot. You were the symbol of adventurous spirit for people like me. You pushed the boundaries of your time much more than I've ever pushed the boundaries of mine."

"But I failed. I got lost. I'm a famous pilot who got lost. I failed to do the one thing I should've done best of all."

"We're lost, too," Janeway said, and smiled. "And we didn't even set out on this voyage on purpose. You, at least, have that. You set out for a goal. Later, others reached it. Part of the idea of adventure is not being sure you'll succeed. Otherwise, there's no adventure, is there?"

Amelia self-consciously grinned. "Suppose not. You know, I'll bet, if I stayed on that planet where I was found, I'll bet I could find my way all around it. If I had more time, I could learn to use some of the . . ."

"The physics?"

"Yes, the physics. I'll bet I could learn theirs fast enough to have myself an adventure or two there."

Smiling again, mostly at herself, Janeway shook her head slightly. "And I wouldn't want to be the one to stop you from trying."

"Thanks," Amelia Earhart said. She stood abruptly and put out her right hand. "Thanks very much. Can I call you Kath?"

"Yes, of course." Taking the hand, Janeway nodded. "You're sincerely welcome. Can I call you Millie?"

Miss Earhart laughed, and her eyes went to bright slits. "My parents called me that when I was a little girl!"

"Yes." Janeway laughed, too. "I know."

Amelia shrugged one knobby shoulder. "Well, again, thanks. I don't care for long good-byes, so . . . good-bye."

With her pride reinvigorated, Amelia Earhart strode out of the starship's engineering area with an air that suggested she would never return, nor would she ever want to. Instead of staring downward at a graph she could never comprehend, she was gazing firmly forward at a future of her own choosing.

The outer door opened, then closed in quiet addendum.

Janeway slumped back, drew the biggest breath she could pull in, and let it out slowly. "I'm sure going to have more respect for the human mind from now on. Did you hear all those details? I only read that file one time! And I can't believe how much better I feel! These melds of yours, Tuvok—what a fabulous tool for therapy!"

Tuvok came forward out of the shadows. "You sense some progress, then, Captain?"

"Oh, yes . . . yes, I do! Oh, I think Amelia would've eventually learned to do some basic technical duties on board *Voyager,* but I understand now that she very likely might've spent her life as a middle-aged curiosity being shown up daily by a crew whose average age is twenty-four. You know, I'm kind of sorry that conversation never really happened."

"It may have," Tuvok postulated, "but in a more subliminal way. Despite your desire to be the one who showed Amelia Earhart the galaxy, you may have sensed her reasons for staying behind. Perhaps that was why you never really encouraged her to come with us. She must have known or sensed what might occur, and that was why she stayed on the planet. There, she still had an entire world's worth of adventure awaiting her, rather than obsolescence aboard the *Voyager*. Captain, I believe, in some small way, I understand."

"So do I," Janeway agreed. She felt as if an anchor had been unstrapped from her back. "At least, I do now. Funny, isn't it, that I didn't before . . ."

Kes moved to the Doctor and looked at the monitor.

A third brain pattern was emerging from Tuvok's. Was it an aberration or combination of some kind?

"A third memory engram?" Kes echoed, as if tasting the concept. "How's that possible?"

"It's not," the Doctor said flatly. "Which means it can't really be an engram." He worked the console for a few seconds, read the results, then worked again. "From the neurochemical modulation, I'd say it's something masquerading as an engram. The way viruses sometimes mimic certain blood factors in order to avoid being destroyed by antibodies."

"You're saying it's a virus?" she asked.

"Whatever it is, it's reacting to the thoron radiation. It's been caused to manifest into an identifiable form. It seems to be an anomalous engram of some kind, some kind of biological agent. But I don't recognize the protein structures. It passed from Tuvok's brain to the captain's. When it did, it created a psychoneural connection between them that was separate from the mind-meld. Their memories are flowing back and forth outside the control of Tuvok."

Kes considered the actions of viruses, almost lifeforms that attempted self-preservation. If this was a virus, and if it would continue to act like a virus—

"If it's acting like a retrovirus in the brain," she blurted, "maybe we can unmask it."

"How?"

"Flush it out with a neurosynaptic surge."

The Doctor lit up to the idea. "Yes . . . but we'll have to modify the procedure to match the pattern of the new engram. If it's an infectious agent, increasing the dosage should drive it out. Increase to forty kilodynes . . . ten-second burst."

Kes started to comply, then said, "Doctor, those are *very* strong bursts. Can their brains absorb that much thoron radiation?"

"We'll see," the Doctor said. "If not, at least they'll be dead instead of in mental anguish for the rest of their lives."

CHAPTER

18

"FIRE!"

Janeway heard Captain Sulu's voice and the plaintive spewing of the ship's energy before her vision cleared. She was on the bridge again.

Clean, this time. Valtane still alive—this must be before the encounter with the three other Klingon ships, but after the encounter with Kang. The *Excelsior* was firing, igniting the sirillium.

Fooom—the blue sparkle filled every screen.

"The Klingon ship's been disabled," Valtane reported. "They're not pursuing."

"Helm," Sulu said, "set a course for Kronos and engage."

Wearing Rand's jacket, Janeway pretended to work a console on the upper bridge. She didn't even know which console she was sitting before. And didn't care.

Sulu glanced at the empty communications post. "Who's at communications?"

Valtane glanced over there too. "Commander Rand's supposed to be on duty, sir."

Sulu parted his lips to respond, but Valtane's console started yipping for attention.

"Sir," Valtane said, "long-range sensors are detecting three Klingon battle cruisers on an intercept course. They're arming torpedoes—"

"Maintain course."

He sat down, and just then the ship was jolted hard by the impact of a fully armed torpedo.

"Return fire!" Sulu ordered.

Valtane tried, then reported, "They've knocked out our targeting scanners!"

"Switch to manual."

Janeway was tense all over, sitting there like a lump while waiting for poor Valtane to die again.

Another hit launched the bridge into a circus of spewing smoke and sparks. Crew members rushed around to assist each other and make good use of whatever was still working.

Valtane leaped up to the science console beside Tuvok. Tuvok was working exactly as he had before, as if he'd never seen this incident before.

Janeway worried about his mental state as she cannily left her post and hurried across the bridge, camouflaged by the jacket she was wearing and the curtains of smoke puffing from various sites of damage.

"There is a rupture in plasma conduit One-Bravo," Tuvok reported, glancing between his console and Valtane's. "It will not hold much longer. Mr. Valtane, there is a rupture in the plasma conduit behind your console—get away!"

Valtane tensed, but kept working. "One more second . . ."

If they were going to fight, they had to have those manual controls. Janeway felt her skin tighten. She'd have done the same thing, and been killed the same way.

"It's about to happen," she reminded Tuvok gently, aware of his delicate mental state. "Try to remember every detail about the next few seconds. Concentrate . . ."

"Dimitri, you must—"

The console exploded in Valtane's young face. Pain and empathy crossed Tuvok's troubled expression. He struggled to keep control as his mind continued to disintegrate.

He crossed to the deck and knelt by Valtane, drawing his crewmate into his arms to ease those last few horrible seconds during which no one should be alone.

Janeway's arms were poised at her sides, but she couldn't move. She sensed something—a presence, a mind—not hers or Tuvok's, but a living presence inflicting itself upon her conscious thoughts. A deep sense of survival came over her, a willingness to fight all those around her in order to stay alive.

"Tuvok!"

The child screamed, then screamed again.

His hand was slipping . . . he had only her fingers in his grip now. He felt one of the fingers break like a twig in his desperate grasp.

The little girl's face was furious with fear. Janeway looked down at her own hand, holding the child's hand, feeling the finger break, feeling the grip lose its traction . . .

"I see her, Tuvok . . . I see the little girl. Stay with it."

"I am trying . . . but my mind is weakening."

"This is our last chance. Go to the precipice. Concentrate on the girl . . ."

"I am trying . . . the emotions are making it difficult. I do not wish to relive the memory again . . ."

"You have to. It's an order. One more time, Tuvok. One more time—"

All right, I've programmed the cortical stimulator. It's working. The mind-meld is almost broken. And the radiation is working on the virus. Increase thoron levels to—

"Kathryn!" The little girl shrieked so hard that Janeway could almost feel the surge of breath through the tiny body. But she couldn't hold on. The girl was wobbling, kicking.

The virus is migrating. It's embedding itself in the captain's brain! Cortical stimulator!

Valtane's body actually smoldered and cast the odor of burning flesh. How much of the pain had he felt? His eyes were open as he gazed up at Tuvok in pitiful plea.

Janeway closed her eyes. The third presence tickled the insides of her skull with a strangely physical sensation. The gopher was burrowing again, trying to push away her own memories to make room for itself. She was on the track of her enemy now.

I can sense you. I know you're here, in our minds. You can't have us. You've had your life. It's our turn now to make the choices. The child is dead. Life has to move forward. You can't have mine or his. Get off my ship.

Her hand was too sweaty. She lay on her stomach at the edge of the precipice, looking down at the child as the little girl screamed, *"Kathryn, help me! Don't let go!"*

But with a sick slurp, the tiny hand slipped through her fingers. Drenched in horror and inadequacy, young Kate watched the child spill away from her. She couldn't hold on! She hadn't been able to hold on, and now the child would die a ghastly death. How could she live with this? How could she live after today?

"Program a fifty-kilodyne burst . . . five-second duration. On my mark . . . now."

He was so young—only a child. Even a Vulcan child is still a child. He couldn't hold on to the little girl's hand much longer.

"Tuvok! Help me—don't let go!"

The sun was so bright, unforgiving—

He has to let go. You have to let go too. You can't hold on to him anymore. I won't let you. Better we fall than serve as hosts to foreign organisms. We weren't built that way. We're individuals. We're strongest when we're independent. Your time is over. Get out. Get out!

It was the twentieth century. She knew, because the little boy was wearing an American Little League outfit and on the ground a radio was blaring the news of an Apollo mission. The boy clung desperately to his little sister's hand as she dangled over the cliff, on the grassy edge of the mountain. Below them, the Shenandoah valley was a cushion of green that would pleasantly kill Karen Lee if he couldn't hold on! He had to hold on to her! He couldn't be the one—

Then his hand cramped. Karen Lee's face broke into shock as she slipped away from him, and fell.

The Masai adults were nowhere nearby and couldn't possibly help him pull Nuta back over the top of the cliff. The bright African dawn pierced his eyes as he tried to look for help, but there was no help. The adults were all working with the herds, driving them away from this cliff where already two calves had been lost. Nuta had come too close, and the edge had chipped away. Now she dangled from his hand, and he couldn't hold on much longer—

"Tukala! Don't let me fall!"

The gods were angry. They demanded a sacrifice, and Chang Li was going to have to make it. He didn't want to—his little sister was so very little yet, and she was his responsibility. Why had he agreed to show her the Summit?

Now she dangled from his shuddering hand, a

thousand feet from the rocky bottom, over the edge where the monks threw their dead goats. She was so small, so frightened. He dug his dirty fingernails into her wrist, but he couldn't hold on . . .

Iacob shook off the terror and ran to the precipice where he had just seen Elishua vanish from his sight. Behind him, his sheep bleated stupidly, not even realizing that a child was in such precarious danger. Was she gone? Had she fallen?

He skidded onto his belly on the edge of the precipice, scratching his muslin tunic. The knot of his rope belt bit into his belly. "Elishua!"

He slammed his arm over the edge and found her arm—she was clinging somehow to the roots and rocks.

"Iacob!" Her voice was so high, so thin!

Panic rushed through the boy. He couldn't hold on. Her fingers were slipping . . .

Get out.

Rameses, pharaoh of Egypt and the Empire, and he did not possess the strength with which to pull one child back over the hungering cliffside. What would the people say? It would become known that the daughter of his sister was allowed to plunge over the side to her death, allowed to die at the hand of a pharaoh-god who possessed no power with which to levitate her back up. Would the people begin to question his powers? His divinity?

He would have to invent a story about gods in the form of wind—

"Rameses! Don't let me fall!"

Muk reached over the edge, barely catching Titi's arm. He bumped the edge of his protruding jaw against the rocks as the child's weight wrenched his shoulder. Before him he saw only the stiff brown hairs of his bare arm and the yellow squares of Titi's parting teeth as she shrieked in fear. The hair on the girl's face rippled slightly as a breeze came up from the stony depths below. Muk's long fingers clenched at her thin arm, but he was losing his grip . . .

At the bottom of the cliff, a herd of mammoths looked up disinterestedly. One of them raised its trunk, waved its huge curving tusks, and trumpeted upward at the proto-human commotion. One of the mammoths gathered its baby under its thick legs, as if afraid that Titi might fall on it.

Muk choked on his own spittle. He was losing his grip—

Janeway reached down and caught at the soft hem of Tuvok's sleeve, catching his wrist just before he would have slipped irretrievably into the open air.

He stared up at her, all Vulcan reserve drained from his chalky face.

She was stretched out on her stomach at the edge of the plateau, her right arm yanked almost out of its socket by his weight—he weighed far more than she did. If she attempted to get to her knees and use the stronger muscles of her legs to pull him up, she'd never be able to keep her grip.

"I won't let you fall," she rasped, her voice scratching out of her throat, raw with dust from the scratching of Tuvok's boots on the face of the cliff.

"Stop kicking . . . we can do this. Keep the grip—don't worry, you're not hurting me . . . I'm not going to let you fall."

"Captain—"

"Try to relax. Brace your feet on the roots. I can see the roots and rocks . . . bring your toes forward, Tuvok. I won't let go, no matter what happens. If you fall, you'll take me with you, and I don't intend to go."

"It's hopeless," he gasped up at her as he dangled. His body slowed its pendulous waving as he took her at her word and stopped struggling.

Janeway tasted the grit of the plateau's edge. "There's something here with us," she choked out. "Something we have to beat together. We can do it, if I don't let you fall and you don't let go."

"But," he wheezed, "is it a life-form?"

"I don't know. I've sensed it for hours—a presence I can't explain. It won't be resolved if I let you fall. It's terrified of letting you fall . . . it's been living with the guilt for centuries, Tuvok. You and I have to beat this entity. All of this has happened with children who couldn't deal with it. We're going to deal with it, you and I . . . right now. Put your toes on the bank and press slightly. Very slightly . . ."

"Captain—"

"Muk!"

"Rameses!"

"Iacob!"

"Tukala!"

"Li!"

"Bobby!"

"Dimitri!"

"Tuvok!"

"Captain—"

"That's it. Your right boot is near a heavy root. Two inches to your center. Don't look down—don't! I'll lose my balance if you swing at all . . . good."

She felt her rib cage bite into the unforgiving stone, felt the ligaments of her arm wrench until her hand began to go numb.

She dug her own toes into the grit and willed herself to stay calm.

"Good," she repeated on a gasp. "Brace on that root . . . I'm going to lower my left hand now. You raise your right hand—"

Tuvok was shuddering every few seconds with mental and physical effort, but he did as she asked. Slowly he raised his right hand to meet her left hand as she extended it.

Her shoulders screamed with agony, but if she inched forward to give herself relief, the imbalance of his weight against hers would yank her over the cliff's edge.

"I'm going to make this our primary grip," she said as their hands took hold of each other by the wrists. "I'm going to pull you up about four inches. Your left foot should be able to reach a little ledge that's at your knee right now."

Dutifully Tuvok didn't attempt to look down, which would have changed the whole attitude of his body as he hung braced on one root and a skinny captain. Janeway summoned all her strength to raise him just a little, and he raised his left leg.

"I have it!" he wheezed with the surge of a tiny win.

"Test it for weight, but don't take your toe off the root yet."

"Yes, Captain . . ."

The ledge held.

"Now, Tuvok, very slowly shift your weight all the way to the ledge. At the same time, I'm going to roll to my right side and pull with the primary grip. Understand?"

"Yes . . ."

"Good. If you don't fall, then our little friend won't have any reason to cling to the guilt. Maybe if I don't let you go," she added, "it *will.*"

"Thank you . . ."

"Ready—rolling."

Grunting with effort, she dug her feet into the dirt and rolled onto her side, levering upward with her left arm, pulling valiantly on his wrist.

In a moment, his black hair made an appearance over the top of the plateau, then his face, limned with effort.

"Find another toehold for your right foot," Janeway instructed, forcing her voice to come out in something other than a series of squeaky gasps.

Tuvok actually had his tongue between his lips as he trembled with every muscle concentrating on reaching the top. Suddenly, his entire left arm flopped over the edge and slammed to the dirt beside Janeway's face—she hadn't even felt her right hand let go of his wrist! That was how numb her arm had become.

"Captain!"

"Out," she murmured as Tuvok winced in pain and hitched himself chest-forward onto the edge of the plateau. "Get out . . . get out . . ."

CHAPTER

19

Consciousness was a funny thing.

Tuvok lowered his hand from Janeway's face. The captain felt the touch slip away. For an instant she nearly snatched out for his hand, determined not to let go.

Had he fallen? Was that why he was slipping backward?

As she watched, he slumped against the back of the seat, his expression exhausted, but calm. His eyes were steady, glazed with revelation, and with relief. He no longer felt the nagging fear of being possessed by the uncontrollable.

Janeway slid back too, letting her shuddering body relax. She hadn't let him fall.

"Are you all right?" she asked him.

He stared at her a moment, then nodded. "Yes . . .

thank you. I am well. You did not let go of me. Most admirable, Captain."

She shrugged, and her shoulders actually ached. "Whatever this was, it clung to the fears of children. I don't know if that was all it knew . . ."

" 'It'?"

"I sensed another consciousness."

Troubled by that, Tuvok muttered, "Indeed?"

"I saw flashes of children holding each other at the edge of some kind of cliff or gulf. They went back hundreds of years, maybe thousands. I saw things like China and Africa and woolly mammoths. Tuvok, this scenario has been playing out, evidently on Earth, for centuries! And I saw Valtane involved in the same scenario."

Tuvok looked stunned. So he hadn't let go of a Vulcan child after all! He hadn't let a little girl die.

"Doctor," Janeway began, pushing herself up, "you got us out of that with some kind of surge, am I correct?"

"Yes, Captain, a thoron radiation pulse drove the foreign organism out of your brains." As he spoke he removed their cortical monitors.

"It was a physical manifestation?"

"Yes, I have it here on the screen, extremely magnified. A most exotic virus."

"Let's have a look."

Gathering their dignity, what was left of it, she and Tuvok shuffled across the carpet, tossing each other a little glance of silliness that they were walking so stiffly, and joined the Doctor and Kes at the small viewer.

Before them on the screen was a bizarre-looking thing that might have been a dot of pollen in another life, magnified many, many times.

"It's clearly a viral parasite of some kind," the Doctor said, "but its origin and genome classification are not on record."

"Probably because it started back so many years ago that nobody even knew about genomes," Janeway commented.

Kes said, "We were able to kill it using the thoron radiation."

"What do you know about it?"

The doctor pointed at the screen. "The parasite thrives on peptides generated in the brain. It evades the body's immune system by disguising itself as a memory engram. I believe it was residing in Commander Tuvok's for the entire eighty years."

"Apparently," Kes added, "the parasite used the childhood memory of the falling girl as camouflage."

"Creating a false memory," the Doctor concluded, "so traumatic that the mind would repress it. And that's where it would live in person after person, hiding in a part of the brain that the conscious mind would want to avoid at all costs. It's a remarkable evolutionary adaptation."

He sounded almost admiring of the clever little . . . whatever that was.

"Well," he finished, "now that we've solved the mystery of Commander Tuvok's troubled past, you're both released. Both your neural profiles are perfectly normal."

Janeway peered at the screen, feeling as if she

ought to give the entity a name or something. Pretty valiant, to stay alive and fight through centuries of human minds, then actually make it out into space.

Had this little thing spawned on Earth? Or had it been brought there by visiting aliens? No such visitation had ever been proven conclusively, but perhaps the proof was lying before her. If this thing could be analyzed and proven not to be native to Earth's biomass, then they'd know, wouldn't they? After all, it couldn't have ridden in on a meteor if it had to have a living, conscious host . . .

So many possibilities!

"When it sensed the death of the host," she went on, thinking, "it would leave to find another." She looked at Tuvok. "That's why it went from Valtane to you."

Kes turned to her. "What about the girl? Did she ever really exist? Or did the organism invent the memory?"

"Memory's a tricky thing," the Doctor said. "If it was a real event, it's been buried and copied and twisted so many times, there's no way to tell what really happened."

"No," Janeway said, "but no monocellular parasite can invent the kind of deep emotional fear and regret as I felt—as *we* felt when that little girl fell over the side. Such a creature might be able to mimic the terror in that child's face or the cloying doubt and guilt, but no one but a conscious, intelligent being can actually create them. Someone, at some time in the distant past, on some planet somewhere, went over a cliff. And someone else had to live with it for the rest of his life. We're the legacy of that moment, and of its very survival. Mr. Tuvok," she said, taking him by the arm, "let's try to get ourselves back to normal, shall we? I'd like to have you join me in my quarters for a quiet dinner. We have lots to talk about."

"Yes, Captain," he said, finally at peace. " 'Lots.' "

The corridor of *Voyager* smelled clean and fresh, reminding Janeway oddly of the scent of the old *Excelsior* in its heyday. She thought of Captain Sulu and how he had tampered with Klingon relations, and held off a half-dozen Klingon ships, giving the *Enterprise* its chance to slip into enemy territory.

"I'm curious," she began as she and Tuvok strode away from sickbay together. "Did the *Excelsior* save Kirk and McCoy?"

"Not directly," Tuvok confirmed. "We were forced to retreat back to Federation space. As usual, Captain Kirk provided his own means of escape. But we did play a pivotal role in the subsequent battle at Khitomer during a second assassination attempt. The same group of malcontents attempted to kill the president of the Federation. Captain Kirk and Captain Sulu headed off the plot in time. I believe they were acting in cooperation all along."

Janeway eyed him cannily. "Mr. Tuvok, if I didn't know you better, I'd say you miss those days on *Excelsior*."

"On the contrary," he told her, "I do not experience nostalgic feelings."

Garbage.

She smiled.

"But there are times," he went on when she paused long enough to prod him, "when I think back to those days, of meeting Kirk, Spock, and the others . . . and I am pleased that I was part of it."

"In a funny way," she said, "I feel like I was part of it, too."

Tuvok offered her a long, penetrating gaze of unknown origin. "Then, perhaps, you can be nostalgic for both of us, Captain."

"Fly her apart, then!"

Captain Sulu
Star Trek VI: The Undiscovered Country

CHAPTER
20

"WARP NINE, MR. LOJUR."

Captain Sulu was visibly subdued, even circumspect, but he seemed supremely satisfied.

At the navigation and weapons station, Ensign Tuvok plotted a course for the Federation-Klingon conference at Khitomer, in Klingon space near the Romulan border.

"Dangerous territory," Kathryn Janeway commented as she stood beside him, still wearing—or again wearing—the jacket she'd appropriated from Commander Rand.

She was pretty sure these people couldn't see her this time, but there was no point taking chances.

Apparently Tuvok saw things that way, for, of course, it was his mind putting the jacket on her.

His mind, slowly being put back in order by hours

of meditation and meld therapy. Janeway wanted to tell herself she was only doing this to help Tuvok wrap up his psychological residue, but in her own mind she was relishing the chance to be here, on this ship, right now. She'd never been much for history, but she needed to witness the end of this affair as much as Tuvok did.

Because all this was somehow necessary to put Tuvok's mind and memories in their correct order— as if she had the foggiest idea what that really meant—she was getting her chance. She would have hesitated, if the Doctor hadn't agreed with Tuvok that more melding was clinically called for, to put Tuvok's mental agitation to rest.

Now, she was getting a chance she'd thought she would never get, almost as if this were as much for herself as for Tuvok.

Around her, she felt the *Excelsior* surge to warp nine. Absolute insanity, Amelia Earhart might have thought. The finest twentieth-century aircraft would have long disintegrated with this kind of physics-defying action.

"Battle stations," Captain Sulu's deep, gravelly voice droned from the command center. "Shields up."

He pushed out of his chair then, and clasped his hands behind his back.

"Put me on the shipwide comm, Janice," he said to Commander Rand, who evidently had a spare jacket in her quarters.

"Go ahead, sir," she said.

"Attention, all hands. This is the captain. We're

heading at high warp to Khitomer on the Klingon-Romulan border. We're trying to meet the *Enterprise*, though they'll probably beat us to that area. Remember what we may be up against—a Klingon bird of prey that can fire while remaining cloaked. These are the same Klingons responsible for assassinating Chancellor Gorkon and framing Captain Kirk and Dr. McCoy. Now, apparently, there's going to be another assassination attempt on Khitomer. These people want to disrupt the peace process between the Federation and the Empire now that the Klingons need help to survive."

Sulu moved forward, and paused on Tuvok's other side, so that he, Tuvok, and Janeway made an unexpected trio at the nav console. Janeway almost moved away, feeling oddly as if she were encroaching upon the other captain's moment of glory.

But she was enjoying herself too much to actually move.

"This bird of prey," Sulu went on, "will likely be running silent, with weapons hot. Once they fire, it'll take too much time to trace the shot back to the ship, even visually. They'll be changing position even before their own hits detonate. They'll probably be using photon torpedoes instead of phasers, to avoid letting us get any straight-line visual references. All stations prepare to relay directly to the bridge anything you pick up on your sensors that might help pinpoint the location of the Klingon ship. Stand by all priority comm channels."

He hesitated, as if trying to think of anything else that could possibly be done ahead of time.

"Captain," Commander Rand spoke up, breaking the peculiar silence that had dropped, "we're receiving telemetry from the *Enterprise.*"

Sulu turned. "Read it out."

"Yes, sir . . . 'To Commander, *Excelsior,* be advised. Klingon ship is standard bird of prey, equipped with unique modifications allowing firing of weapons while maintaining cloak. Believe possible—'" She paused, frowned, plucked at her controls, then turned to Sulu. "They've been cut off, sir."

A tremor of excitement blew across the bridge.

"Well, if they know anything we don't know," he said, "we'll have to find it out some other way."

Janeway leaned to speak to Tuvok. "What could cut them off? Jamming from that cloaked ship?"

"Yes," Tuvok murmured quietly. "They were . . . they *are* being headed off by Chang near Khitomer. With his modified bird of prey, he is a strong match even for a starship. And we have no way of knowing whether or not he will have summoned any other support ships."

"At warp nine," she murmured back, "we'll find out pretty darned soon."

"Sir," the Halkan at the helm began, "coming up on the Romulan-Klingon border. Khitomer is showing on my long-range chart."

The ship whined and shuddered around them without respite, an endless vibration that went down into her structural bones. The groan of plates about to pop was a tooth-grating sound, and Janeway found herself squint-eyed and clench-fisted as she stood beside Tuvok. He glanced up at her, and there was decided fear in his eyes.

So strange—he knew he would survive, but the fear was still there.

After a few calculated moments, Sulu asked, "In range?"

"Not yet, sir," Lojur said, dark eyes reflecting the glow of the main screen.

"Come on, come on," Sulu chanted, possessed. "Increase speed to—"

Lojur swung around in his seat. "She'll fly apart!"

Sulu's glare turned vicious. "Fly her apart, then!"

His roar cut everyone off at the throat. The whole bridge crew suddenly lunged to their own consoles, as if no one else wanted to have that tone used toward him or her.

Poor Lojur turned back to his helm, wide-eyed, slack-jawed, and humiliated.

In admiration Kathryn Janeway stared at Captain Sulu. He not only took this chance—he begged for this chance. He was furious that one more dilithium crack of speed might not be attainable, that one more inch of forward movement might be out of reach. Better to die in a ball of flame than play it safe and arrive to find a charred husk where the *Enterprise* had been and a smashed conference with the littered corpses of dignitaries rotting in the sun.

What a moment!

"Almost there," Lojur croaked, his voice failing him.

"Weapons nearly in range of Khitomer system's spatial sphere, Captain," Tuvok reported.

Janeway felt a shiver rattle down her arms. Yes, she was there for Tuvok's sake, to finalize the reordering of his mind, to file these memories into the right order and relegate them to the past, where they belonged, but she also felt she was there for herself. A visit to home space, a chance to witness these intrepid forerunners in the last great effort they shared, to feel this tough old-style ship around her and notice how strong they could build a long-range ship, even then—yes, all this was good for her too.

"Sir," Tuvok spoke up, infectious excitement tightening his voice, "I have the *Enterprise* on scanners."

"Acknowledged." Sulu moved to Lojur's other side, closer to Rand on the upper bridge. "Send to commander, *Enterprise,* from me—'The cavalry's here!'"

"Aye, sir, sending!"

"Sir, reading a firing signature—no source," Tuvok choked out, taken by surprise by his own instruments.

"The Klingon ship!" Lojur blurted. "I don't see anything on these instruments!"

"We expected that," Captain Sulu said calmly. "Hold course. Reduce to impulse speed the instant you're within firing range. Everyone settle down. We have to be very workmanlike in the next few minutes, but be ready."

"Aye, sir," Tuvok said.

"Aye, aye, sir." Logur, Rand, and two other bridge personnel echoed.

"The Klingons are firing on the *Enterprise,* sir,"

Tuvok said, deliberately keeping control over his tone, partly because he was Vulcan and partly because he'd been ordered to.

Janeway glanced at him, but instantly put her glare back on the main screen. Now she could see the *Enterprise*—Kirk's *Enterprise!* The crew with more accolades than any other in Starfleet history lay before them in slightly battered but beautiful form, her brilliant saucer blistered with damage, her upward-swept warp nacelles raised like a swan's wings. She was a lot sleeker than Janeway had ever picked up from models or holograms.

"I can't get a fix on the Klingon ship," Lojur said, frustrated and tense even though he'd been warned that this might happen. "Dropping to full impulse speed, sir."

"Shields up. All right, now we're giving them something else to shoot at."

"Aye, sir!"

"Veer directly toward the *Enterprise.*"

"Aye, sir."

Janeway tensed as a photon torpedo appeared out of apparently dead space and launched toward the *Enterprise,* which took the hit with a quick, last-second dodge to port, allowing the photon to strike a hard but glancing blow. Still, the starship held position and continued an almost leisurely arch of forward movement.

"The *Enterprise* is making itself a target," Lojur voiced. He turned to Sulu. "Why, sir?"

Sulu settled again into his command chair. "If I know Captain Kirk—and I do—it means he's figured out a way to tease the cloaked ship into revealing itself. Mr. Tuvok, you be ready to fire at the slightest opportunity. I don't care if you empty the banks with near misses."

"I understand, sir," Tuvok said, and glanced up at Janeway.

She nodded approvingly at him, and clenched her hands, aching to take physical part in this.

"Sir, they're firing on us!" Lojur called out as a bright ball of energy popped out of empty space and blew toward them.

"Evasive," Sulu said.

Lojur tried, but the bolt was too fast and thundered into *Excelsior's* primary hull just in front of the bridge. Janeway winced. Another few hundred feet, and there wouldn't be anything left to remember.

"All stations, stabilize or evacuate," Sulu said. "We'll clean up later."

Smoking and sparking, the *Excelsior* continued to close the distance between itself and the *Enterprise* and the ship nobody could see. As they approached, another bolt popped out of the fabric of space and streaked toward the *Enterprise*.

Tuvok stiffened. "Sir, the *Enterprise's* shields are severely damaged."

"The *Enterprise* is returning fire," Lojur called out sharply. "How are they targeting a cloaked ship?"

"Any way they can," Sulu droned. "Hold fire . . . wait a minute. Keep your eyes open, people. Mr. Tuvok—"

"Standing by, sir," Tuvok said with unexpected enthusiasm.

Janeway leaned toward Tuvok as they watched the *Enterprise*'s photon torpedo speed through space. "Why did they fire? They can't possibly have a solution plotted for an invisible ship."

"Wait, Captain," Tuvok said.

As they watched, the glowing orange dot of the torpedo streaked into space as expected. Then, quite unexpectedly, it began to loop around, banking quite deliberately.

"That warhead's acquiring!" Lojur gulped. "How's—it's tracking the cloaked ship's ionization trail!"

Behind Janeway, Sulu smiled and murmured, "Mr. Spock . . ."

Janeway glanced at him, realized what he meant, then watched the screen with renewed fascination.

The orange dot drove back around the *Enterprise* as if framing the starship, curving artistically against the sun's distant shimmer, then lazily circled, but not a full circle. Soon it straightened its course and no longer acted erratic.

"Did it lose the cloaked ship?" Janeway asked.

Wisely, though, Tuvok didn't tell her.

"That Klingon ship stands between us and Khitomer," Tuvok said instead, "where this same group of conspirators is about to attempt assassination of the president."

"If just one of these two starships can slip through—" Janeway gripped the back of Tuvok's chair and fixed her eyes on the screen. She was suddenly glad not to know exactly what had happened at this moment in history.

The torpedo made one more course adjustment loop, then increased speed quite suddenly.

"Captain," Tuvok said quickly, "it might be inside the cloaked ship's neutron radiation sphere."

"It's surging for the hit!" Lojur gasped.

"Keep your eye on that warhead, Mr. Tuvok," Sulu said. "We'll only have a few seconds . . ."

"Aye, sir."

Tuvok didn't take his gaze from the screen. He who had so firmly argued against coming into Klingon space at all would be the one to deal the final blow, and he seemed glad to be doing so. His shoulders were tensed and he was leaning forward, both hands on the controls, his eyes hungry for the action to come.

The *Enterprise's* glowing orange photon torpedo increased speed to maximum, and its tight maneuverability made it deadly, even to a hidden ship. No ship could bank out of the way fast enough to avoid that thing.

Janeway felt her face flush in the light of the strike. An empty square of space buckled and spat debris and illuminants, flashing the shape of a Klingon bird of prey as the ship fell out of cloak.

She drew in a quick breath—she'd never seen one of those in person. Arched wings and a broad cyclopean head growled out of the darkness.

What a stealthy, mean-looking ship! Of course, the Klingons designed it that way.

How very different it was from the battle-forward brightness of the *Enterprise*.

Behind her, Captain Sulu barked, "Aim for the center of that explosion and fire!"

Tuvok did the quick targeting, then moved his hand to the firing controls. At the last instant he looked up. "Captain, you do it."

Janeway blinked, realized what he'd said, then reached out and pounded the fire control. Certainly *felt* real . . .

Two torpedoes launched from *Excelsior* at her touch, and she felt as if the power were surging down her arm and through her fingers to the enemy ship.

The *Enterprise* fired again, too, two bolts also, but the *Excelsior's* bolts reached the bird of prey first, just as the Klingon ship was trying to fade to invisibility again. A plume of sparks blew from the spine of the foam-green ship, as if Janeway had shot an arrow and struck a flying vulture.

The second bolt hit a wing and caused the ship to bobble downward to port as if wagging in space to signal someone.

The *Enterprise's* bolts cut into the Klingon ship's back and neck and severed it, but the pieces had no chance to drift apart before *Excelsior* fired again and hit the other wing.

At last the *Enterprise* dealt the death blow to the Klingon ship's main section. The bird of prey's engines imploded and critical mass defined itself in a shock of expanding gas and light and a puff of chemical cloud.

Drenched in its own gushing atmosphere, the

bird's head snapped upward as if sledgehammered in the neck, but before it could fold back on itself, the skull blew into a sparkling sphere with a nearly audible *pop*.

Debris shot through space in every direction, chased by the fireworks of uncontained energy.

Janeway stared at the screen with undisguised amazement. She was shocked at the power-packed nature of that vessel. It must have been nothing but engines and weapons, with maybe a little air to breathe. Maybe.

"The bird of prey is destroyed, Captain," Lojur said with great satisfaction. "The way to Khitomer is cleared."

"Follow the *Enterprise*," Captain Sulu said. "Let them arrive there first."

"Aye, aye, sir!"

Janeway knelt beside Tuvok at the helm and let the flicker of destructive power play across her face. She placed one warm hand on Tuvok's arm and relished the personal contact.

"Tuvok," she uttered, "thank you! But it's only a memory, you know."

He looked up at her, quite warmly this time. "To you and me, Captain," he said, "it will be history."

"Only a fool fights in a burning house."

Kang
Star Trek: Day of the Dove

CHAPTER
21

"MR. PRESIDENT!"

A shout throbbed through the reception hall, shaking every dignitary to the bone.

Kathryn Janeway, though she had expected what was about to happen, flinched against her own tension. Her hands were drained and cold. She felt as if she were the only person in the theater who knew John Wilkes Booth was about to fire.

In today's case, the assassin was disguised as a Klingon, and hiding high in a loft instead of a balcony. But the president did have a beard.

She beamed in beside Tuvok not far from Captain Sulu. Before she even had a chance to turn, she heard the shot of the phaser rifle and the contained gasp of the crowd.

The hall was crowded with delegates, ambassadors of numerous planets, wearing different-colored sashes to identify each delegation's representatives.

To the left, several Starfleet officers were herding certain people to the center. Janeway started to look in that direction, when Captain Sulu snapped, "Cartwright!"

When she turned to look, Janeway saw him aiming his phaser—at a Starfleet admiral!

"Just a minute," Sulu ordered, keeping his phaser and those of his security team in the face of the shocked admiral.

Seemed he was right. The admiral was trying to skirt out of the hall while everyone else's attention was turned inward.

Only now did Janeway recall that there had been upper-echelon Starfleet personnel involved in the conspiracy. Every race had its fingers in the mess— everyone had a stake, one way or the other, in the standing or collapsing of the peace.

At the podium, the president of the United Federation of Planets was being lifted to his feet. Janeway enjoyed a moment of awe for the thin, tall albino Deltan with long snowy hair and a Fu Manchu beard and mustache. He had come down in history as the best president since Abraham Lincoln.

Perhaps that was why she had been thinking about John Wilkes Booth.

Standing custodially beside the president was a Starfleet captain with sandy brown hair and a squarish face. Janeway only needed a moment to recognize him.

"James Kirk!" she breathed. She'd seen him in log

reels and heard his voice, but this personal experience was heartwarming.

He had just saved the president's life, and the assassin now lay on the floor, blasted out of the tower by Kirk's chief engineer, Montgomery Scott, who was just now arriving on the lower level. Not far away, Dr. Leonard McCoy had a phaser up the nose of what looked like a Romulan.

And there—the legendary Mr. Spock, the first Vulcan in Starfleet, was pulling along a young Vulcan Starfleet officer, a woman. He seemed most stern, but somehow satisfied.

Stunned delegates gawked as somebody pulled a Klingon mask off the assassin.

"It's Colonel West," somebody proclaimed.

A human. The conspiracy could claim all lands.

"What is the meaning of this!" a Klingon woman demanded.

At Janeway's side, Tuvok leaned to her and said, "That is Azetbur, daughter of Gorkon and the new chancellor. The Romulan is Nanclus, ambassador and conspirator."

"It's about the future, Madam Chancellor," James Kirk said, oversounding Tuvok's murmur.

The captain's voice was distinct and familiar, more mild than Janeway would have expected, his enunciation particularly good, yet somehow very normal, subdued and approachable, without a touch of pretension.

Well, maybe a touch.

"Some people think the future means the end of

history," Captain Kirk went on. "Well, we haven't run out of history just yet. Your father called the future 'the undiscovered country.'" He faced the new chancellor and said, "People can be very frightened of change."

The young Klingon woman fought to think past her own fears as she anchored herself in the captain's eyes, the eyes of the man who had fought Klingons all his life and now was fighting to save them. Perhaps it was unthinkable to these people, back then, that one civilization should stick its neck out for another, even if they'd been enemies for as long as anyone could remember.

With some inner resistance, Azetbur accepted. "You've restored my father's faith."

With tolerant radiance, Kirk's eyes grew soft. For this moment, all the legends of the hard and unbending man of war lay down before another persona.

"And you've restored my son's," he said evenly.

The sense of joy, of strain and grief, rippled through the hall. Someone began to pat his hands together. Then someone else. In moments, the crackle of applause rose to the high ceiling.

Summoned by the applause, James Kirk moved to the riser behind the podium, and was joined gradually by Captain Spock, Captain Sulu, Captain Scott, Commander Uhura, and others Janeway hadn't yet come to appreciate.

"Thank you, Tuvok," she uttered. "Thank you for letting me share this."

"You are welcome, Captain," he said, his voice

betraying an inner warmth he would have otherwise denied. "You are most deeply welcome."

The junior officers' quarters were unoccupied, but for one contemplative Vulcan and a quiet observer. The lights were dimmed in recognition that the quarters had recently lost an occupant to death in the line of duty, more or less an in-board method of lowering the mental flags to half-staff.

Lieutenant Valtane's burial in space would be staged in the main bay at sixteen hundred.

Meanwhile, Tuvok was packing. Slowly.

The door chimed, and he hesitated before saying, "Come."

He turned and seemed perplexed when Captain Sulu strode in. "Hello, Ensign."

"Sir . . . good morning."

"I received your transfer request. I see you're packing to leave the ship." Sulu casually hitched up to sit on the nearest study desk. "I hope it wasn't over the disagreement we had."

"Only partially, sir. I have requested reassignment in preparation for leaving Starfleet and returning to Vulcan."

"After all the time you spent at the Academy?" Sulu wondered. "That's a lot to throw away. I've seen your records. You were a fine student."

"Most Vulcans are 'fine' students, Captain."

Sulu openly laughed in agreement with that, a throaty whole-body laugh that filled the cabin. "Yes, yes, they are. So, can I talk you out of leaving?"

Tuvok seemed troubled. "I doubt you can, sir.

However, I would not be so rude as to keep you from trying."

Sulu smiled and folded his arms. "Well, good. Are you sure it's not because of the incident we've just been through?"

"Not directly, sir."

"Then . . . your behavior on the bridge, maybe? You may have been a little out of line, but I understand you believed you were following regulations. After all, I *was* bending interstellar law."

"Yes, sir, you were."

Sulu grinned passively and glanced around the room, as if trying to think of more to say or just killing time.

"Was that incident embarrassing to you enough to make you leave Starfleet?"

For the first time since his captain entered, Tuvok stopped covering the moment's unease with packing his duffel. "Not entirely, sir. After all, I do believe I was right."

"You were. But at the wrong time. Happens to the best of us. You just haven't figured out which times."

"Captain—"

"Let me tell you what I think," Sulu interrupted. "I think we need more Vulcans in Starfleet, not fewer. Did you know you were assigned to the bridge because I personally requested a Vulcan up there?"

Pausing in contemplation, Tuvok seemed to have been genuinely take unaware by that one. "No, sir . . . I had not been aware of that. I appreciate that and regret that I did not perform adequately."

"You did fine. We just disagreed. Maybe it's just

nostalgia on my part, I don't know," Sulu said openly, "but I think Vulcans bring a great deal to Starfleet. Are you sure you've given yourself a chance to find that out? I've noticed that Vulcans tend to be hard on themselves. If you'll agree to stay on board for another stint, you and I can have some conversations. I can tell you some sea stories about Captain Spock. And a few tall tales of my own. One of them involves bringing a sword to the bridge."

He bobbed his brows playfully.

Tuvok shifted uncomfortably, clearly not under-standing what his captain was doing here engaging in small talk and not seeming at all ready to leave.

"I am not sure I can accommodate you, sir," the young Vulcan said. "My discomfort is most pro-found."

"Everybody's is, at first," Sulu told him. "You should give yourself more of a chance. You've only been aboard a short time. I realized it's a little harder for Vulcans to feel as if you fit in, but believe me, you do."

Tuvok paced a few steps away from the bunk, contemplated the wall briefly, then turned.

"Perhaps we are just not compatible. Humans and Vulcans, in a space environment, I mean. I truly feel I should go back to Vulcan and study, seek out my own inner qualities and talents, and decide where I will be of most value in my life."

Sulu shrugged understandingly. "No different from the rest of us, Ensign. Don't forget that. I think more Vulcans should join Starfleet. We need you.

Not just for your rigorous logic, but other things. Together, I think we're stronger."

The two fell silent for a moment, and during that time Captain Sulu should have gotten up to leave. After all, the conversation had run its course.

Oddly, though, he stayed right where he was, sitting on the desk with one foot swinging a little, his arms folded, and his shoulder pressed to the edge of the mirror.

Tuvok clasped his hands behind his back and waited, not having the slightest idea of what to do or say next. Perhaps this was just a time to stand at parade rest and let the officer decide what would happen. And a Vulcan could stand at parade rest for a heck of a long time.

Captain Sulu had an odd smirk on his face, as if he were thinking of a joke but not telling it.

"What time is it?" the captain asked then.

"Thirteen sixteen, sir."

"Ah. A minute late."

"I beg your pardon, sir?"

The door chimed again then, and despite the fact that this was Tuvok's cabin, Captain Sulu invited, "Come in."

The panel parted, and a looming presence entered the half-light. Narrow and imposing, the uniformed figure filled the doorway briefly, then stepped in.

"Glad you could make it," Sulu greeted, and finally pushed off the desk. "Captain Spock, this is Ensign Tuvok."

"Good afternoon, Ensign." Captain Spock's voice

was heavy, low, laden with his years of experience, and surprisingly at ease. "Captain."

"Captain," Sulu returned, faking the formality and still smirking. "Thank you for coming. How is everything on the *Enterprise?*"

"Quite well. The captain and Dr. McCoy suffered no ill effects of their incarceration, and the conspirators have been remanded to Starfleet Headquarters to be charged with the assassination of Gorkon and the attempted assassination of the president. The peace accords are progressing with renewed vigor, I might add."

"I'll bet. If you'll excuse me."

"Certainly."

"Ensign, perhaps we'll talk again." With a nod, Sulu glanced at Tuvok and then headed for the door and left quite unceremoniously.

Spock was a dominating presence, though he was as subdued as fog. He made no pointless gestures or movements, but gazed at Tuvok with a certain contemplative dispassion. Though they seemed to understand each other, at least on some basic level of courteous behavior and expectation, the air of tension in the room was noticeably heightened.

"A difficult decision," Captain Spock began, as if he had been there all along. "I remember my own."

Menacing in his way, Captain Spock seemed mannerly, pacific, but with undercurrents of expression that he wasn't afraid to have seen, even by another Vulcan. Evidently, he was past that. Every phrase carried a subsense.

"I have learned great admiration for humans," he

granted. "They have accomplished a great deal despite the chaos of their emotions."

"Accepted," Tuvok endorsed. "However, no matter the level of efficiency and accomplishment among them, I have discovered that I have difficulty fitting in. I do not believe I can contribute here. If I am continually awkward in my comprehension of humans, and cause confrontations of the sort—of a sort that will upheave already tense situations, then I am in fact . . . detracting from the ship's efficiency. There are now occurrences which I cannot ignore."

Spock nodded with his own personal style, and straightforwardly said, "You may speak freely, Ensign."

Taken by surprise, Tuvok evidently thought he *had* been speaking freely.

After a few seconds, though, he did find something to say. "Thank you, sir." In spite of the gratitude, Tuvok remained deeply disturbed at admitting the core of his troubles. "I bordered on mutiny today, sir, in this latest event that turned out to be so critical in keeping peace. I recognize now that if I had been successful in my protests to Captain Sulu, the ship would have turned away from the challenge, the *Enterprise* would have been destroyed, and the galaxy would be at war this very minute. I proceeded cautiously and logically and followed regulations, yet was still entirely wrong about the outcome. Captain Sulu's decision was completely irrational, yet completely successful. As we look through history, these irrational decisions often turn out well. I do not believe I could make decisions that way, or go along with decisions made that way. If I cannot fit in, then I cannot contribute effectively. I will be a part of the machinery that fails at a critical moment."

Maintaining his image of a sedate pillar, Spock neither nodded nor in any way proclaimed what he was thinking about that. He gave neither approval nor chiding to Tuvok at this difficult time.

He took a few long seconds to think about his response, and, curiously, didn't seem hurried. That was a strange Vulcan-to-Vulcan trait which many learned not to do when among humans, who frequently interrupted each other in conversations. Vulcans, when speaking to each other, seemed unfazed by long periods of silence for thought.

When Spock broke the silence, the flow of fine diction was decidedly passionate.

"I entered Starfleet to escape the kind of tensions which you have found here. As a half-Vulcan, my turmoils on Vulcan were more stressful than those I found in Starfleet. I had some internal conflicts, of course, but having been raised on Vulcan I have always considered myself Vulcan. Yet, I found my fellow Vulcans intolerant not of my behavior or intellect, but of my blood. The very illogic of that drove me away, to Starfleet. When I found discomforts there, I had nowhere to escape. Therefore I stayed until I was much older than yourself. My deepest questions came rather later in my life."

"You had questions," Tuvok said, "yet you are still in uniform."

"*Back* in uniform, Ensign. I did leave, for quite a

while. I, too, abandoned my Starfleet career to study the Kohlinar. I found it informative, but ultimately static. I cannot tell you that things that seem irrational are true, though you know they are not. I can suggest that you will learn to adjust yourself. Your logic will encompass more than itself someday."

Though Tuvok tried to appear hardened and unmovable, summoning the hardheartedness that Vulcans often fell back upon, he hesitated for several telling seconds before asking, "Captain, are you recommending that I remain?"

Spock, on the other hand, never hesitated. "Quite the contrary. You should leave Starfleet and go to Vulcan to purge your dissatisfactions."

Another pause, but a different kind.

"I do not understand," Tuvok said, letting his guard down a little. He evidently wanted an answer even more than he wanted to be left alone.

"You should go," Spock explained, "because your doubts will fester otherwise. You must explore all your avenues. Should you come to change your mind," Spock continued, "you should know that no one at Starfleet will begrudge your leaving. It is my sincere hope that you someday consider returning. There are certain types of knowledge that go beyond logic. Diversity is not possible in the homogeneous environment of Vulcan. We can preach diversity, but we cannot experience it if we reject that which is diverse. Logic is linear, Ensign. Life is not."

Another significant pause was disturbed only by the clatter of ship's business out in the corridor as a maintenance team rattled by with some kind of cart.

"That is," Tuvok said eventually, "logical, sir."

"Yes, of course." Spock appeared amused to the untrained eye. "I will tell you what I tell many young Vulcans, and hope to someday rekindle your curiosity. Logic can be a shackle forever holding you back, or it can be a platform from which to begin your investigation of life and the lives around you. It is a starting point. Little more."

He broke his stance, which had until now seemed very casual, with an even more casual movement toward the door, and there paused.

"I will leave you now," he said. "I wish you satisfaction, Ensign. Live long and prosper."

"Thank you, Captain. Live long and prosper."

The door breathed, and closed again. Tuvok stared at it for many seconds.

From the deepest corner, in a place where she could sit on a dim bunk and watch these conversations, Kathryn Janeway stood up and moved forward.

How deeply was Tuvok involved in this last bend in the labyrinth? Would he be aware of her?

He had to be. Even if he wasn't, it was time.

"You've been lucky," she stated, without reminding him of her presence in any more subtle manner. "Counting me, of course, you've had some very profound captains on your side."

He didn't look up at her. "Yes. I regret that I failed to fully appreciate them until they were gone." Quite abruptly, then, he raised his eyes to her. "I am glad, Captain, that you are still with me. If I had to be banished to the far reaches of this quadrant, I am pleased to be here with you."

He didn't wait for her to answer or indicate with his posture that he expected an answer, though she thanked him with a smile and waited, sensing that he wasn't finished.

He sighed with obvious relief, paced across the room, gazed through the mirror at his own clasped hands, and seemed at peace for the first time since the blue nebula had appeared on *Voyager's* scanners.

"Spock's words always stayed with me," he told her. "I remembered for fifty years that I could come back if I chose to. When I abandoned the Kohlinar to raise a family, that choice was girded by Spock's advice about accepting change for the good. Had he and Captain Sulu not quite illogically and impolitely interfered in my moments of decision, I may never have considered marrying, or returning to Starfleet. It took me fifty years to rejoin the fleet, and eighty years altogether to understand these memories. I am gratified to put this conversation with the captains in its proper order. While I will never abandon my basic philosophy, I do believe my logic is more encompassing now. I have been learning to mesh with you and other non-Vulcans. I have discovered that, though I have not admitted it to myself until now, it does give me a certain satisfaction."

"Well," Janeway said, "I'm glad. You're out here in the middle of uncharted space, without any chance of retreating to Vulcan. You have to live with us, no matter how uncomfortable it becomes. But,

Tuvok, we all do. Remember the phrase 'No man is an island'? Let me tell you something—we're *all* islands. We're all separate and different and utterly alone inside our skin. It's only how we learn to accept, handle, or grapple with each other that dictates how the horizon will look every morning. And you know what else? It never looks the same two mornings in a row, Tuvok. Not to me and not to you. It's important to appreciate that daily difference."

Bridging the moment to what inevitably had to come, she stood up and took his arm.

"Between you, me, and Amelia Earhart," she said, "I'm almost glad all this had to happen. But let's get back to reality, shall we? We've got a lot of horizons in front of us, you and I. I think it's time to start heading forward again."

"Captain's log, Stardate 9529.1. This is the final cruise of the Starship *Enterprise* under my command. This ship and her history will shortly become the care of another crew. To them and their posterity will we commit our future. They will continue the voyages we have begun and journey to all the undiscovered countries, boldly going where no man . . . where no one has gone before."

Captain James Kirk
Star Trek VI: The Undiscovered Country

CHAPTER
22

LIEUTENANT COMMANDER TUVOK ENTERED THE SHIP'S
mess hall with some measure of pause. He told
himself he hadn't been avoiding this place, but he
knew better and was poor at self-deception.

The crew glanced at him, but most were cautious
and did not approach. He was hardly surprised,
given the chain of events to which they were all still
so closely linked.

Yet something was different as he gazed out over
the crew, almost all humans. He felt more comfortable here than usual. Despite their cloying glances,
he sensed an underlying care in their eyes and
warmth in their disquiet.

How different this was from those weeks aboard
the *Excelsior,* during which he had felt only lack of
understanding and disapproval, yet he had had no

right to disapprove but his own Vulcan arrogance. Jealousy, he decided. The humans had accomplished so much in only a few generations, while the Vulcans languished in studious isolation for centuries.

He had discovered in the years between that he would rather be part of the accomplishment.

All these people were willing to risk themselves for him, and Captain Janeway and Kes were willing to go into the most unbelievably foreign territory, the territory of the mind. Such ground was strange enough for a Vulcan, much less for creatures of emotion. The ship and its troubles, Chakotay and the others, all thrust into turmoil, yet had controlled themselves and worked the problems through without sacrificing him, which certainly would have been his own consideration. All had been willing to risk everything for him.

Ah—Neelix.

Creeping toward him, Neelix emerged from the galley, shoulders hunched, chin tucked, eyes sorrowful.

"Mr. Vulcan . . . I'm . . . so glad to see you."

"Neelix," Tuvok greeted immediately, glad to have the first hurdle jumped. "I know what happened. I understand your position, and I agree with you. Risking Kes along with the captain was inexcusable. I would have . . . chosen termination had I known."

"Oh, no—" Neelix clasped Tuvok's arm. "I never really wanted that. That's what we were all afraid you'd do."

Tuvok paused, seeing the guilt riddling Neelix's face and bearing. Suddenly he understood that guilt. He had experienced it through the actions of the memory virus, and now saw that Neelix was experiencing guilt despite having done the right thing and making a perfectly logical argument.

Now that he knew what it was like, he began to regret that humans, Talaxians, Ocampas—all these creatures of top-floating emotion—had to bear guilt at all.

"I bear you no ill will, Neelix," he said, mustering his version of warmth. "I have found there is something to learn from charging into new experiences. You, all of you, so effectively deal with emotion rather than running from it. There are certain advantages you have in handling feelings rather than banishing them. I owe my life to that determination. I know that in the past months you have made my comfort your personal mandate, and I have rudely resisted your efforts. But now," he said with an unexpected sigh, "I realize I should be more open to new things, just as my captain and friends fearlessly strode into danger on my behalf. Even into things that are not logical at all. Emotional beings seem to try newness for its own sake, and are almost always charged by the result."

"And we would all do it again for you," Neelix said, more quietly than usual. "I was just . . . so worried about Kes."

Tuvok nodded. "I know you were. After eighty years, I finally understand *why* Captain Sulu risked the ship and his career as he did, going in to save fellow crewmen when it would make more sense not to. Neelix, I would like you to aid me in learning how to do this. Perhaps we can start simply. Here, today. I will try any culinary experiment you wish to attempt."

Neelix's whole posture changed. "Oh, Mr. Vulcan! You've made me so happy! I won't let you down, believe me! I'll try and try until I find some way to make Vulcan dishes for you just right! I'll experiment day and night!"

"Thank you," Tuvok said. "But also . . . I will try any non-Vulcan dishes you create. After all, Neelix, the goal is to widen my horizons. Perhaps, with gradual conditioning, I too can learn to risk everything for the right reason."